Praise for *The Chemist of Catania*

"Not since Ann Radcliffe has a British auth
portrayal of Southern Italy. While written entirely in English, Fr Alexander
Lucie-Smith's new novel somehow achieves the rhythm of Italian prose....
The novel has the fundamental building blocks of a good story, believable
characters and a solid moral message.... Unlike the sex and violence now
so gratuitously depicted as to lack any novelty, everything is purposeful in
Lucie-Smith's storytelling.... These moments are vital; they will shatter the
illusions of anyone keen to excuse the horrors of organised crime which
continues to grip many parts of Italy and the world beyond." Georgia
Gilholy, *The Catholic Herald*.

"I was greatly impressed by your handling of the large cast of characters,
the rich sense of place and, above all, the universal air of corruption that
emanates from its pages. Calogero must be the most inveterate teenage
villain since Pinkie and, unlike Greene, you don't give your central
character even a hint of redemption. The perverse sexuality and
pervasive sadomasochism add to the novel's powerful mephitic air. And,
of course, you beautifully capture the impotence and compromises of the
clergy." Michael Arditti, novelist.

"An unexpected page-turner... The remorseless amorality of the anti-hero
should make him completely unlikable yet somehow I joined the book's
characters in finding him interesting and a little compelling. I loved the
slow character-building as gradually the younger brother emerges from
the shadow of his criminal elder to shine hope towards a better future.
The author also understands the compromises that generally good and
well-meaning people will all-too easily make when faced with an
immovably powerful and corrupt force in the shape of a pivotal individual.
So this is more than just a crime potboiler, it is a really interesting
reflection on a society where amoral behaviour flourishes - for a time at
least - and of the sheer logistical difficulty in bringing it to book. A real

moral parable for the realities of the modern era, in many cities and countries, not just the one he describes." Ruth Gledhill, journalist.

"I was quickly drawn into Alexander Lucie-Smith's tale of an odious young Mafia-type gangster, Calogero, in *The Chemist of Catania*. It follows this bad hat's tyrannising career, evoking the fatalism of Sicilian society, the efforts of a well-meaning priest, Don Giorgio, the passivity of the womenfolk. The probing of sin and the interplay of conscience with survival are brilliantly handled. You need to know what happens next." Mary Kenny, summer reading recommendations, *The Tablet*.

From Amazon:

"Mario Puzo eat your heart out, Lucie-Smith knocks your book into a cocked hat."

"The author's style of writing had me wanting to know more at every step of the way."

"Gripping read."

"Couldn't put it down."

"Lucie-Smith not only manages to perfectly convey the claustrophobia of this rancid little town, with its eagle-eyed overlord forever watching the people in the square below and plotting his next swoop; he is also a master fable writer, and the tale is rich in symbolism."

"Clever, complex, atmospheric."

"Very enjoyable, exciting read."

"The setting in Sicily is authentic and the research has clearly been thorough and enthusiastic. Very many successful and popular series of detective novels set in Italy are available, whether written in English, or translated from Italian. And the best are very good indeed – for instance the Inspector Montalbano series by the Italian Andrea Camilleri who died in 2019 and the Aurelio Zen series by the English writer Michael Dibdin who died in 2007. Those who have enjoyed them may be seeking a new series. Help is at hand!"

"*The Chemist of Catania* is a riveting tale about crime. From page one you are there, in Catania, which is brilliantly realised, as is Messina, where a later scene unfolds. This writer clearly has Sicily and Itay in his blood, and the reader catches his enthusiasm. The characters, both major and minor, are memorable. Calogero, clever, malevolent, cruel, but also disturbingly compelling, almost sexy, dominates, but people like the lawyer Petrocchi, the priest don Giorgio and the younger brother Rosario are convincing and fascinating. The plot moves fast, and one knows that it won't lead anywhere good: this is a book about people who are utterly amoral, who will do anything to get what they want, and the compromises and cowardice of good people who feel unable to stop them. The inventiveness of the plot is quite breath-taking, and the twists and turns are matched by arresting turns of phrase, which never descend into mere literary showing off. 'The lion roars at noon,' we are told of the Messina clock tower. This novel roars on every page. I loved this book and cannot wait for the sequel."

"With its gripping plot, authentic setting, and morally complex characters, *The Chemist of Catania* offers a chilling exploration of ambition, corruption, and the brutal consequences of pursuing power at any cost. Highly recommended!"

"A page-turner from start to finish. Wonderfully written, characters that come to life superbly and a fantastic plot."

"A real page-turner, and a lucid account of the behaviour of the people of the extraordinary and appalling Mafia in Sicily."

"Like any good novel, it leaves you wanting book 2!"

"Compelling."

The Chemist of Catania

a novel by

Alexander Lucie-Smith

Chapter One

The Quarter known as Purgatory lay close to the centre of Catania, not very far from the Via Etnea in one direction, or the railway station in another, and only a short walk away from the Cathedral and University squares. It took its name from the church at its centre, which was dedicated to the Holy Souls in Purgatory. This once gracious building, rebuilt in grand style in the second half of the eighteenth century, was the property of a confraternity of medieval foundation, whose purpose was to pray for the souls of those in purgatory. The Ancient and Noble Confraternity of the Holy Souls had prospered under the Bourbons of the Two Sicilies, and been lucky enough to escape suppression under the various anti-clerical regimes that had replaced them. The Church, like the rest of the quarter, was in need of repair; the apartment blocks in the quarter all suffered from leprosy of the façade, and some were in a state of partial ruin; and yet there was something beautiful about the little quarter of a few streets and one principal square, for those few adventurous outsiders who dared to visit. In the square, after the daily market was packed away, boys played football; in the bar, the older men would play board games under the shade of the solitary tree that grew near its door, a large spreading Mediterranean oak. It was here, in a flat not far from the square, that Calogero di Rienzi grew up, with his mother and his father, with his two sisters, and with his younger brother, Rosario, who was four years his junior.

By the time he was twelve, Calogero was a big child, almost able to pass for an adult. He dominated the football players of the square, who deferred to him, and if they did not, paid for it. He won every fist fight he entered, and he was not squeamish in administering punishment to those who offended him. One boy, in an incident that everyone remembered, had his nose broken against the front step of the Church. That sealed Calogero's reputation as a boy no one should contradict.

By the time he was twelve, his mother, who was deeply religious, was in awe of her son; Rosario, then eight, simply feared him. His father viewed him as a promising character. This man, who was later known only by the name of 'The Chemist', for he was a former science teacher, specialising in chemistry, like many Sicilian fathers, worked abroad, and came home from time to time. The Chemist would come and go irregularly, and his wife never asked him about his work. He would take the train north, and disappear for a week, sometimes two, sometimes three. His work would take him to Turin, or Milan, or Rome, it was assumed, or further afield, to Belgium or to Germany. This was the way things worked in Sicily. The father of the house was absent, and no one asked where he went, though it was clear that his work was remunerative. The family owned the flat they lived in, which was relatively spacious. Moreover, signor di Rienzi carefully invested his earnings in other properties around the quarter. By the time Calogero was twelve, he had already persuaded the owner of the not very profitable bar to sell up; and the owners of other run-down properties he had his eye on were always open to persuasion. Calogero's father hardly ever spoke at length, and he certainly never smiled, or so Calogero noticed whenever he accompanied his father on his rounds. He had an aura of authority that made people want to co-operate, and which Calogero envied. With his father, the boy would go and collect the rents once a month, and he watched people pay up with alacrity, not wanting to offend the Chemist. Some of the properties were dingy single rooms on ground floors, with doors open to the street, which he realised were rented by prostitutes, women no longer young with ruined faces for the most part, and in a few cases teenage males only a few years older than himself, whom his father treated with pronounced disdain. Those who did not pay on time were evicted without any warning, their possessions and themselves thrown into the street, amidst the general curiosity of neighbours and indifference of passers-by. Calogero helped with these evictions whenever they arose. He noticed when still young that no one ever intervened to help the victims; no one liked the unfortunate; they were the sort of people who made others instinctively turn away, reminding them perhaps of the bad luck that could befall anyone. And such bad luck! To end up on the pavement weeping, your face stinging from the Chemist's slap, surrounded by your possessions and your clothes, with the Chemist's son looking at you with wry triumph.

Calogero learned his lessons well, and by the time he was fourteen he acted as his father's rent collector, while his father concentrated on his work abroad, and invested the profits in an ever-expanding list of properties. Purgatory, during these years, was still a slum, awash with uncollected and stinking rubbish, a place with a reputation for danger, a place that the guide books to Catania warned you to avoid. The Chemist, however, gradually evicted many of his old tenants and replaced them with a better class of person who could pay more and who required less management. Also during these years, the years before the second Berlusconi government, the Confraternity, which owned the Church of the Holy Souls in Purgatory, began to finance a complete restoration of the exterior and the interior, saving the building from possible collapse, and bringing it to the attention of those who loved architecture. The Confraternity was feeling the benefit of the economic revival of the city, reliant as it was for its income on the rents from several buildings along the Via Etnea.

Though his father trusted Calogero, he never confided to him what he did when he went abroad. Calogero had become a skilled thief by the age of ten. His curiosity about how his father made his money led him to search for whatever evidence he might find. But his father's wallet revealed nothing at all, and his father's unpacked suitcases on his return revealed nothing either. Nor did his father have a mobile phone or a computer. This in itself was highly suspicious: after all, everyone had a mobile phone, nearly everyone had a computer. And many adults had plastic cards in their wallets – but not his father. On one occasion, he had accompanied his father to a travel agent in the city and watched him buy a train ticket to Naples with cash, and cash, he knew, was untraceable.

Again, he was intrigued to know just whom his father worked for; but there was no one he could ask. Accompanying his father on his rounds, he paid attention to whom he met. Most of his calls were of a commercial nature, to collect rent, to check up on tenants. But one or two did not fit into this category. There were several trips, for example, to a hardware shop in the Via Vittorio Emanuele, where the rather tired and sad proprietor was one signor Vitale; a man a few years older than his father who seemed wedded to terminal discretion. Vitale and his father would discuss very little: a consignment of this fertiliser had come in; there was a shortage of nails or screws; it was as if they were speaking in an elaborate kind of code. And his father usually left, after a prolonged visit, without buying a thing. Given that he did not have a garden and never did anything of a practical nature in the house, it was never quite clear what business he might have had with signor Vitale. But signor Vitale was some sort of link to the outside world, the world beyond Catania. And he got his much younger friend Turiddu to follow his father, and see where he went. Turiddu confirmed that the hardware shop was a frequent calling place.

It was hard to discern a pattern, but by the time he was sixteen or so, Calogero had the distinct idea that the visits to the hardware shop in Via Vittorio Emanuele were co-ordinated with his father's trips to the other side of the straits of Messina. In other words, Vitale was the one who arranged and directed his father's work, or passed on messages and directives from those who did. But what was that work? Naturally he noted the dates of his father's absences, and he scoured the newspapers and watched the television news for unusual events that might coincide with the Chemist's trips abroad.

In the end, as he progressed through his teenage years, he developed several theories as to what his father did, and did so secretly. First of all, he imagined that his father might be working in some capacity for the government, perhaps as an undercover policeman. When he walked through the city with his father, the Chemist often stopped to talk to certain policemen, whom he spoke to as to old friends. Was he himself a secret policeman, a secret bodyguard for some important politician? But this seemed too fantastic to be true. Moreover, he knew that his father, like himself, disliked and distrusted authority of any kind. By the time he himself had discovered the pull of sex, he began to assume that his father led a double life and that somewhere in Italy there was another family, another wife, another set of children, and that his father was a bigamist. Given that he was away more than half the time, this seemed an attractive theory.

Was there a parallel family? Was there someone like himself, who imagined himself to be an eldest son, in some place like Reggio, or Bari, or Rome? Every man needed a wife, it was part of his status as a man, but could his father be one of those unusual men who needed two wives? And if that were the case, would he keep them unknown to each other? Wouldn't one have been the wife, and the other the mistress?

In the end, he thought his father an unlikely bigamist. For a start he knew that his parents were properly married, as he had seen the marriage register in the Church of the Holy Souls in Purgatory. Don Giorgio had shown it to Rosario, when Rosario was just starting out as an altar server, at the age of eight, and when he heard this, Calogero had asked Rosario to show it to him too. There it was, clearly set out, that Renato and Maria di Rienzi were married in church, and one could not do that unless one proved that one were single first. But that really did not prove anything more than a putative second marriage was second in time as well.

By the age of fourteen Calogero was an adult in his own eyes and in the eyes of the rest of the quarter. He had had his first sexual experience with Anna the Romanian prostitute, who was one of his father's tenants, the previous year. He had noticed her as the most beautiful of all the women, prostitutes or not, in the quarter, and thought her a useful conquest with which to begin. She had a young son, and had only arrived in Catania a few years previously. He had met her when collecting rents on behalf of his father. At first, she had refused his advances, which had only made him more insistent. Finally, she had given in, and in the dingy ground floor room she rented from the Chemist, allowed him to have what he wanted in return for the unspecified goodwill of her landlord's son. Everyone else had to pay fifty euros.

He kept up with Anna for some time, and was a regular visitor. He liked the cachet that she brought him, the fact that he did not pay, was not even asked to pay, that he was in a different class to the rest of the quarter. He liked the transactional nature to the encounters, their lack of emotion. He even enjoyed the way Anna clearly resented him, found his visits an imposition. It reinforced his sense of power. As for the other boys and men of the quarter, they were jealous, which pleased him.

Of course, Anna complained to his father about his attentions, and his father had ignored her. Or so he supposed. He guessed his father knew, for from that time onwards, because he was now a man, his father stopped beating him.

On one occasion, walking through the square Turiddu, the younger boy had drawn his attention to the child with curly dark hair, who was Anna the Romanian prostitute's son. The child, knowing them both, had looked up from where he sat on the church steps. Turiddu had gestured towards Calogero and said to the boy: 'Yesterday he fucked your mother.' Calogero had seen from the boy's expression – he was only seven – that he understood what this meant. He shrugged, and then gave Turiddu a slap in rebuke, a hard one too; he noted that the little boy realised that in Turiddu he had an enemy, but in Calogero a possible friend.

While he kept up his relationship with Anna, he also began to pursue a girl called Stefania, who also lived in Purgatory. She was the most attractive girl of his age group, and her family was of a slightly higher social status than his own, he knew. Her father had regular employment, and her mother had social ambitions. Of course he liked her, but what particularly amused him was the way her family and she herself were torn by the prospect of him becoming her young man. They clearly sensed that he had a future, an interesting future, but they wondered about the risks this future might involve. She was keen, and they were keen, though keen to hide it as well, lest they give the indecent impression of pushing their daughter into his arms. As he saw more of Stefania, he visited Anna less; his sense of propriety dictated that when he started sleeping with Stefania, he should stop sleeping with Anna.

He did have a sense of propriety. He recognised what was due to Stefania when she became his official girlfriend. She added to his prestige and the respect in which he was held. The idea that he should have two women at the same time seemed to him not just extravagant, but unnecessary, and he doubted his father had ever thought in such extravagant terms either.

His relationship with Stefania, more than his experiences with Anna the Romanian prostitute, marked his entrance into the real world, the adult world. Not only had all corporal punishment ceased by the time he had become Stefania's young man, but his father was markedly more generous to him financially when Stefania arrived, and gave him a car, whereas previously he had made do with a scooter. He drove it for two years before passing his test. By this time too, he had ceased to go to school (he was never officially expelled, but the school was grateful for the absence of so impossible a pupil) and he certainly never went to Mass, not even at Christmas and Easter, following his father's example. His father exercised no restraints on him; his mother had long ceased to imagine that she ever could.

His mother, a devout woman, was saddened by the way he had grown up so quickly, but this, she felt, was the usual fate of mothers, or so she reasoned. He was an eldest son. With Rosario, for whom she had always felt markedly less affection, it would be different, and it was different. And with the girls, Assunta and Elena, too. She would have been dismayed had she known just how her eldest son passed his time when he wasn't collecting rents for his father, or fornicating with Stefania, which is what she imagined he was up to at night. However, most nights when he was not at home, he was with Turiddu, committing robberies.

He had long had a natural aptitude for locks. This was something his father had taught him. He was able to pick any lock – sometimes there were locked cupboards and rooms left behind by evicted tenants, which had to be opened. Sometimes tenants thought they were clever and changed the locks. But he could get through virtually any lock, car locks the easiest of all. Car radios were simple to steal, and there was a market for them, for petty local criminals were always on the lookout for them, and would ask the local boys from Purgatory if they had any to sell. The next best thing were wallets, and here Turiddu, who started out on this career just after his First Holy Communion, was invaluable at distracting tourists in the Cathedral Square while Calogero lifted their wallets. This resulted in a profitable harvest: there was ready cash, which the boys kept for themselves, while selling the wallets and the cards onto the same men who bought the car radios.

The stolen goods were kept in Turiddu's bedroom, which was his exclusive domain, being the only boy in his family, and where Calogero had free access. Bit by bit, the two youngsters graduated onto better things. Calogero, though intelligent, had learned very little at school apart from an appreciation of art. It did not take long for him to realise that the city's churches were poorly guarded. He was not so unsophisticated to look with longing at the contents of the poor box. He preferred the sight of the silver candlesticks on the gradine of the altar. Most churches had a custode, whom one of the boys could distract, while the other filched the candlesticks, or dipped into the sacristy and took a silver chalice.

All this might have come to an end when Turiddu was ten and Calogero fourteen, and Turiddu's father discovered the stash of stolen goods in his son's bedroom. The boy was given a terrible hiding. Calogero found him the next day, snivelling and bruised on the steps of the Church of the Holy Souls in Purgatory. He soon extracted from the boy what had happened, and marched Turiddu up several flights of stairs to the family home and rang the bell. Turiddu's father answered. He was not a small man, but he was not much bigger than Calogero. Calogero floored him with a punch to the jaw, and then administered a good kicking, without a word being said. The boy's mother rushed out of the kitchen screaming. She pleaded with him to stop, but Calogero continued until the man was unconscious and his own shoes were covered with blood. Turiddu watched knowing that his father would never hit him again. Then Calogero left.

He returned the next day. The battered and bruised father opened the door and Calogero was pleased to see the fear immediately apparent in his eyes. Turiddu appeared in the background.

'Turi,' said Calogero, 'Get your father's keys.' The boy did as he was told. 'Take off the cellar key, and makes sure you get me the spare ones as well.'

Calogero took the keys. He was now master of the storeroom in the basement, which had a secure metal door. Moreover, he had sealed the humiliation of Turiddu's father, who would never dare mention to anyone how he had lost his cellar to a mere fourteen-year-old. The cellar was now his, and with it a place to keep the stolen goods. He already knew what he had to do next. The greatest trophy of all awaited him.

He shared a room with his brother Rosario, who was used to him coming in late and had even trained himself to pretend to not wake up when Calogero came in at two or three in the morning. The ten-year-old Rosario knew better than to antagonise his older brother in any way. A child of little interest to their father, the matter of disciplining Rosario was farmed out to Calogero. The slightest complaint – such as at being woken up in the middle of the night – would win swift retribution. This was not because it was wrong to complain or because the boy had to be taught a lesson; it was rather because it delighted Calogero to see his younger brother live in the fear of saying the wrong thing, and consequently live saying virtually nothing at all. To further terrify and discomfort the boy, the physical cruelty was interlaced with moments of extravagant affection, so that the ten-year-old boy never quite knew where he stood or what to expect. Every time Calogero came into the room, Rosario would be beset by an agony of uncertainty.

That night, a night he would remember, the night that followed the day on which Calogero stole the cellar storeroom from Turiddu's father, he sensed that Calogero had entered their shared bedroom quietly without turning on the light. He heard him undress, as he pretended to be asleep, with his face turned to the wall. He had to get up early the next morning, because he was serving Mass at the Church of the Holy Souls in Purgatory at 6.30am, and it was his job to open the Church for don Giorgio, the priest, and get everything ready for the Mass. He had to get up in time, and get up quietly, without waking his brother, which was always stressful. Then Calogero got into bed; but not his own bed; rather he pushed his supposedly sleeping brother nearer to the wall, and got in next to him, something he had a habit of doing from time to time. Rosario felt his brother's arms around him, and his breath against his neck, and he knew he would not sleep for hours until his brother left him alone.

'Go to sleep, go to sleep,' said Calogero, who had felt him stiffen.

He knew he had no choice but to pretend to be asleep, if that was what his brother wanted.

Round his neck he wore a gold chain which had been given to him for his first Holy Communion, which held a cross; and the brown scapular of Our Lady of Mount Carmel, which he had vowed never to take off. He felt his brother playing with the gold chain and the cloth of the scapular, and the third cord around his neck on which he kept the Church key, so that he might not lose it. His brother fiddled with these chains and cords, as if

16

pretending to strangle him; at the same time, he was stifled by the smell of Calogero, which reminded him of liquorice, but was in fact the remains of the perfume that Stefania wore. He realised that his brother had set himself the dare of trying to steal his cross and chain, his most prized possession, or else to remove the scapular, that sign of his dedication to God and the Blessed Virgin. He knew too that there was nothing he could do about it, and that he would have to spend days, weeks, even months, pleading with Calogero to return the treasured items, which would be taken, he was sure, just to torment him.

After a moment, he surrendered, and allowed Calogero to do whatever he wanted. It was easier that way. Later, Calogero left him alone, and he fell miserably asleep.

Dawn came and with it the deepest relief. He had trained himself to wake up at first light, without the help of an alarm clock. He woke, and found that he was mercifully alone. Moreover, the three things with which he had gone to sleep were still round his neck. And so he had run off joyfully to the Church of the Holy Souls in Purgatory, opened the Church with the key with which don Giorgio had entrusted him, and set up for Mass. The Mass, that morning, was being celebrated on one of the side altars, as the main altar was obscured by scaffolding and plastic sheeting, thanks to the restoration project, which involved cleaning the marble and the gilded wooden frame that surrounded the altarpiece, the Spanish Madonna. Indeed, the Madonna was so obscured that it was not for another week that anyone noticed that she was gone; and even then, for a few days the restorers assumed that one of their number had moved the picture from its place in order to facilitate the restoration. Only after an afternoon of raised voices and recriminations, between don Giorgio, the head of the Confraternity, and the restoration people, was it clear that the Madonna had been moved without authorisation and that her whereabouts were unknown. In other words, the picture had been stolen.

The interested parties, the priest, the restorers, the police, the Confraternity, the people of the Purgatory quarter, could agree on virtually nothing at all, except that this was a disaster of the greatest magnitude.

For the police, it was the greatest embarrassment imaginable. The painting was the only Velasquez in Sicily, a gift to the Church by the wife of one of the Spanish Viceroys in the mid-seventeenth century. While not much known outside the city, it was one of the more important paintings in Sicily, and certainly one of the most important paintings in Catania, which, unlike Syracuse or Messina, could not boast a Caravaggio of its own. But there was no clue who could have taken it, no evidence of forced entry, and it could not even be established when the painting had been removed. The high altar had been covered up for weeks.

Don Giorgio was the custodian of the Church, and felt that he was responsible. The Madonna should have had an alarm fitted, or should have been removed for safekeeping; he feared he would be blamed, and in order to cover up his sense of negligence, he blamed the restorers. They came and they went at all hours: they were lax about keys. Perhaps they had left the Church open, perhaps they had tipped someone off, or perhaps they themselves had stolen the picture. There were so many thefts from churches of late, and so many restorations; the two were connected. But there was no proof at all, and all this succeeded in doing was offending the restorers, who quit en masse, and considerably delayed the restoration project in the process.

The Confraternity, who owned the Church and its contents, were mortified in the extreme. They saw themselves as guardians of the city's cultural heritage, and now they had lost their most valuable possession, which made them a laughing stock. Moreover, the picture was not insured against theft, thanks to some oversight. The Confraternity met. It had about 600 members, of whom never more than a dozen usually turned up for meetings, but this time several hundred assembled, and vented their rage on the head of the Confraternity, an elderly Duke, who had inherited the position from his father, and who was forced to resign, to be replaced by a middle class but efficient lawyer called Petrocchi, a man who would, it was hoped, make sure things like insurance were taken care of in future.

As for the people of the quarter, they were distraught. The religious ones, who were relatively few, and overwhelmingly female and elderly, were shocked that people should steal from churches. They knew there were thieves about – Catania swarmed with thieves – but these thieves should leave their churches alone, and something bad would happen to them for their sacrilegious profanity. The more superstitious saw the vengeance of God fall not on the thieves, but on the quarter itself, which had now lost its heavenly protectress. All of them had been baptised or married in her presence (the painting was not an it but a her). Her benign oversight had guaranteed their happiness in the past; who would look after them now? The cult object was gone and the temple was empty; now the Church was just a useless building which served no purpose. This attitude, which he heard repeatedly, angered don Giorgio. Did these people not believe in God, and the sacraments, and the scriptures? Did they only believe in a picture, albeit a holy one? Had they forgotten Jesus in their enthusiasm for Mary? And in what sense could the people of the quarter be said to love the Madonna they now mourned, given that they spent their time in fighting, swearing, fornicating, prostituting themselves and thieving, all of which were most repugnant to her heavenly purity?

In the end, said don Giorgio crossly to himself, it was only a picture. A very good one, it was true; a valuable one and a historically important one, but what really mattered remained; but the people of Purgatory by and large did not seem to understand what really mattered. They were children. The idea that God would abandon the Church just because the Velasquez was gone struck him as infuriating, and made him realise just how little they understood the spirit of Catholicism. It depressed him. He was living among pagans.

Eventually, after an interminable and inexplicable delay, the police began to ask who had keys to the Church of the Holy Souls in Purgatory. The answer was not comforting. There were about thirty keyholders: sacristans, altar servers, members of the Confraternity, the cleaners, the restorers. Rosario was questioned, albeit briefly, and he told the truth: he kept the key around his neck and he never took it off.

But of course someone else had taken it off, and that someone was now, the boy could tell, extremely pleased with the theft he had pulled off. Moreover, Calogero had a partner in crime, Turiddu, a boy the same age as Rosario, who now carried himself in the manner of someone much older and much more knowing. This conspiracy of thieves, his fourteen-year-old brother, and his ten-year-old accomplice, was present before Rosario's eyes, knowing what they knew, and knowing too that he had been used by them and dared not say so.

In the end Rosario saw that he was responsible for the loss of the Spanish Madonna; and yet, how could he have prevented it? What could he have done? His brother had taken him by surprise, and taken advantage of an opportunity Rosario had never foreseen or even dreamed could have existed. And what had become of the painting itself? The newspapers and the television reports were adamant that the painting would soon resurface and be returned, because the thief would try to sell it on, and the police who safeguarded the artistic heritage of Sicily (a job they had not done so very well) would find the painting before it left the country. The Madonna was too immediately recognisable to be sold without detection.

This opinion was confidently stated as fact; and yet, as the months passed, the Madonna did not resurface, and new and insistent rumours arose. It was, it was said, adorning the stateroom of a Russian oligarch's yacht; it had been burned by a desperate thief who could not sell it on; it had been fed to pigs belonging to a crime boss from somewhere near Palermo. This last supposition became the favoured legend of the police and of the people of Purgatory. The crime had been committed to make them all look stupid. The criminal had taken the painting, not because he wanted it, but to prevent them having it, and to show up the police for the fools they were. Moreover, the theft of the painting was an enduring insult, given that when the restoration of the interior of the Church of the Holy Souls in Purgatory was complete, above the high altar, encased in a baroque effusion of gesticulating angels and fluttering putti, all newly gilded, was a black hole where the Velasquez had been. The whole Church now had no real purpose, designed, as it had seemed to be, to showcase the picture. The sight of that hole filled Calogero with triumph; true, he could not sell the picture on for now, as he realised that would be far too dangerous; but the black hole reminded him of his power to make other people suffer. The same hole filled Rosario with the most tremendous guilt. He knew that pigs had not eaten the canvas and that it was not on the yacht of a rich Russian. He knew his brother had taken it, and he knew too that there was nothing he could say, as he was complicit in his brother's crime.

Their mother, like the religious women of the quarter, was despondent about the missing picture. Their father, the Chemist, who had been away at the time of the theft, never said anything about the matter, but seemed thoughtful, and sometimes Calogero caught him looking at his eldest son with interest, and wondered if he knew.

Chapter Two

The reputation of the Purgatory quarter as a place of crime and disorder, and a place where you should never park your car, was cemented by the tale of the theft of the Spanish Madonna. Many had hoped that the restoration of the Church would help the quarter to become more prosperous by attracting tourists. But if any tourists ever came, it was to gawp at the scene of Catania's most mysterious and audacious theft, and they ran the risk of being robbed of their wallets by teenage boys, or of their car radios if they were foolish enough to park nearby. Visitors did come to the streets of the quarter, but usually for a bad purpose, to visit the prostitutes who worked out of the lodgings let to them by Calogero's father. The Chemist, as his sons grew to maturity, was still frequently absent, but growing richer; and Calogero himself too was growing fat on the proceeds of petty crime. The gang of teenage boys he controlled brought in several wallets a day, for which they were rewarded; in addition, Calogero was not averse to extorting money, supposedly as loans, from the prostitutes and other tenants too; the contents of the wallets were sold on to other criminals in other parts of the city. And then there were the stolen goods from churches, which, with the sequestrated Madonna, were in the metal-doored storeroom in the basement of the block of flats in which Turiddu lived. These were kept securely as an investment against the future. For Calogero had a plan, and thought ahead. He imagined an important future for himself.

The beginnings of that future happened when Calogero was sixteen, and Rosario twelve, two years after the kidnapping of the Madonna. One sunny October afternoon, leaving school, Rosario was met by his elder sister, Assunta, and knew at once that something was wrong. No one ever met him from school, and he had walked on his own to school since shortly after beginning his education. His sister explained.

'Something is happening,' she said. 'The police have come round to the house and are there now, asking mamma questions.'

'What do they think she has done?' he asked.

'I don't know. Nothing, I imagine. She gave me a look which told me to come and get you. Or at least to warn you that they were there. I think – she wasn't able to say – the police are waiting for Caloriu to come home, and she wants you to find him and to warn him.'

'Are they going to arrest him?'

'How should I know?' asked Assunta crossly.

Indeed, how should she? Her brother's affairs were his own. She had no knowledge of them at all. She had never asked, never wanted to find out; never felt the slightest twinge of curiosity. It was better that way. It was a way that she had learned from her mother. But this lack of knowledge angered her. She was a year older than Calogero, but she counted for nothing, because she was a girl. Rosario did not quite understand this, he merely noticed that she was perpetually cross.

Rosario knew what he had to do. He had to find Calogero. The arrival of the police in the quarter was unprecedented. He was sure he had never seen any member of the various police forces in the quarter in all his twelve years of life. But the arrival of the police in the family home, this was simply unthinkable. It could only mean that they were there to arrest Calogero, that he had been found out. Their father was absent, which perhaps meant they had chosen their moment to pounce. He knew he had to warn his brother, so he could run. But where would he run to? Of course, he could hide out in the quarter, where the police could hardly search every flat, every room, every tenement. They would never catch him. But should he warn his brother? Why not let him be caught, let him be arrested, let him be taken away?

As he walked back towards Purgatory, the thought of a world without Calogero became real to Rosario. If they arrested him, the nightmare would end. The malevolent presence would be gone. But if he were to betray his brother, he was sure his brother would find out, if not immediately, then eventually. And his revenge would be terrible, for he would have committed the dreadful crime of family disloyalty. After all, Calogero, whom he hated, was his brother, and the police were nothing to him. And yet, the police, if they had come to arrest Calogero, surely had justice on their side. But the prospect of turning in his brother frightened him. What if any police enquiry into the theft of the Madonna narrowed it down to his key? What if he had to spend the rest of his life knowing that his brother would one day surely punish him for his crime? He knew what was right, but he did not know whether he had the courage to do what was right.

It was 3.30pm, and Calogero, who was usually up all night, would be asleep somewhere, he knew. His first call was to the house of Stefania and her parents, to see if he were there. He knew the parents would be out, and he knew too that his brother slept with Stefania, and he had always imagined this took place in the quiet of the afternoon, so Stefania's flat was the obvious place to look. He rang the bell and was admitted, and walked up several flights of steps; but though Stefania was there, Calogero was not. The only other place he could think of was the house of Turiddu on the other, even poorer, side of the quarter. Once more, he rang the bell and walked up several flights of stairs, and was admitted by Turiddu's sister, who like himself had just come in from school, and said that she thought Calogero might be with her brother in his bedroom. He approached the bedroom door with trepidation, and knocked. There was no reply. He knocked again. He was just about to try the handle, when the door opened a crack.

It was Turiddu, the boy whom he so disliked and to whom, before now, he had scarcely ever spoken.

'What?' asked Turiddu crossly, but in a low voice.

'I need to speak to my brother.'

'He is asleep.'

'It is an emergency. The police are at our house and we think they are there to arrest him.'

'Let him in,' came Calogero's voice.

Turiddu opened the door and let Rosario in. The room was dark and fetid, a room that had been well slept in. Turiddu was wearing his underpants, and now began to search the floor for various items of clothing which he began to put on. Calogero was in bed, and looked at Rosario with annoyance at the interruption.

'I was up all night,' he said wearily.

Rosario told him what had happened. Calogero became attentive, and his demeanour altered. He was suddenly tense. Of course, people did go on the run, did become outlaws. Was he destined to be one as well? But if they had come to arrest him, then what was the charge? What had they found out? Who had betrayed him? One thing was sure. He would not go home until he was certain it was safe to do so; he would not go home until he knew more. He looked at his brother with the knowledge of one who knew he had to rely on him and that no one else was available.

'You go home and try and find out what has happened, why they have come. Tell them nothing at all about me. You do not know where I am. You do not know where I might be. When you have found out as much as you can, then come back here and speak to Turi. I may not be here, but Turi will know where to find me. Try not to be too long, but remember, when you come back here, don't lead the police here. Understood?'

Rosario nodded. His brother had by now jumped out of bed, all hint of sleepiness dissolved, and was searching urgently for his clothes in the mess on the floor.

'What are you staring at?' asked Calogero, now pulling on his jeans. 'Get going and report back.'

Rosario ran home, and when he got there he found his mother and his two sisters sitting at the kitchen table, and opposite them two men in plain clothes. He knew, as soon as he entered the room, that someone was dead. His mother had that monumental aspect to her; she was totally still, as were Assunta and Elena. They were not grief stricken, at least not yet; they were stunned. His mother's face was expressionless, void of feeling; the two girls were looking at her with concern, as if waiting to take their cue from her. Rosario put his school case down very carefully, so as not to make a noise, as if any noise might somehow disturb this utterly still scene, as if any noise might trigger an avalanche of grief. Then he went and kissed his mother on the cheek, which was cold; she made no response, and gave no sign of recognition that he had entered the room.

The two policemen looked at him: the older one with grave seriousness, the younger one with an expression of sympathy.

'Did you know your husband was in Milan, signora?' asked the younger one gently.

She shook her head numbly and dumbly.

'Did he tell you what he was doing there?' asked the older one.

'He never spoke about his work,' said Assunta, not without bitterness.

'Had he telephoned?'

'When my father is away, he never telephones,' said Rosario, feeling he ought to speak, and to spare his mother and sisters. 'He comes and he goes and he never bothers us with details.'

'Do you know what your father did when he was away?' the younger one asked Rosario, who noted the use of the past tense.

He shook his head. 'I don't ask questions,' he replied. 'My father did not welcome questions. What has happened?'

'I am afraid your father has had an accident,' said the younger policeman. 'He is dead.'

'But to me,' said Rosario's mother, bursting into tears, 'he was good man always'.

'But not to others?' asked the elder of the policemen.

Rosario put a hand out to his mother, without looking at her, keeping his eyes steadily on the two policemen. 'Don't speak, mamma,' he soothed.

It occurred to both policemen immediately that there was nothing to be gained from prolonging the present conversation; indeed, there was no conversation worthy of the name. The two girls had learned their lesson early and learned it well. One did not speak to strangers. Their father did not even speak to his own family. The young boy knew nothing; and even if he did know something, he would not speak.

'Where is your other son?' asked the elder of the two policemen. 'He should be at home right now, shouldn't he? Is he at school?'

But no one seemed to know where Calogero was. The mute misery in the room made it all but impossible to discuss the whereabouts of Calogero.

The two policemen rose to leave, nodding to the signora, acknowledging her grief, and that of the two girls. Rosario saw them to the door, as politeness dictated.

'You had better go and find your brother, son,' said the elder of the two as they left. 'Is he a bit older than you? Yes? Then your mother will need him.'

'What has happened to my father exactly?' asked Rosario.

'He had an accident. Your mother will explain.'

They disappeared down the staircase. Behind him, Rosario could hear the first sounds of sustained grief from the kitchen. They chilled him. Today had started like any usual day, and now it was to end like this, in the theatre of grief and ritualised mourning. He could see it all – the visits by relatives, the funeral, the burial, the family tomb, the eyes of the whole quarter on him and his sisters and his mother and Calogero. And Calogero, at the age of sixteen taking the place of his father. But for his father, he felt nothing at all. There was a blank where the grief should have been. He had been away so much. Then last week he had gone away again, and now he would never return. How would they manage without him?

Having ascertained that the police had left, he ran down to the street and ran the short distance to where Turiddu lived. The door buzzed and he ran up. Turiddu was at the door of the flat.

'Is he here?' he asked. 'No? Find him and tell him that the police came to tell us that our father is dead. He had an accident in Milan. That is all I know. They were not looking for Caloriu at all. They do not know who he is. Caloriu needs to come home at once. My mother is very upset.'

Turiddu ran the length of two streets, and came to an open door; he ran to the top of the staircase and knocked on the door. It was opened by Anna the Romanian prostitute. In the single room behind her he saw Calogero, lying on her bed, with her son next to him. The small boy, with his dark curly hair, was reading to Calogero from his First Holy

Communion text book. Turiddu delivered the message. Calogero became immediately pensive, while Traiano, the boy, kept on reading regardless.

Rosario walked home slowly, and only a few minutes after his arrival his brother caught up with him and entered the flat. His manner was grave, and already he was a changed man, someone who was preparing to take charge. His mother looked at him, acknowledging his new authority. She gestured to the two girls to take Rosario away. Then Calogero closed the kitchen door. His mother then told him what the police had told her. His father had been killed in a hotel room in Milan the day before. They had had difficulty identifying him. He had been blown up. A bomb had detonated. They had not said anything, but the implication was clear. Signor di Rienzi had been killed by a bomb he was making or a bomb he was carrying.

Calogero took this in. It all made sense. His father had been a trusted man, someone important. He felt a sudden thrill at the realisation. No wonder they had paid him well. But now, he had failed, and that failure had cost him his life. The people he had been working for might be annoyed by that. Clearly they valued discretion above all else: and how secretive his father had been.

But that discretion had come at a price. He acknowledged to himself that he felt nothing for the dead man, his father. They had never spoken, they had never known each other. His father, in leading a hidden life, had used his children and his wife as a disguise, as camouflage. He had used them, and felt nothing for them. So what could Calogero feel for him, now that he was dead? And what did Calogero feel for anyone? He felt as he sat in the kitchen opposite his mother a double feeling: an interior emptiness coupled with a desire to get busy and be doing things. His father was dead: there was much that needed to be done.

His sisters would look after their mother, and so would Rosario. That would be their role. In a moment he would call them into the room and tell them so. Then he would phone the lawyer, and speak to him, tell him the news: of course, he knew, having made the rounds with his father for years, just what the family owned, and he knew who the lawyer was. It would be necessary to make sure all the paperwork was in order. All that would be relatively simple, he was sure; his father would have left his affairs in order, for he had always taken care that everything was legal.

But there was something else, something more personal to be done. He would have to go back to that hardware shop in Via Vittorio Emanuele and try and find out what had really happened. The people who had employed his father were people he wanted to speak to, and perhaps signor Vitale in the hardware store was his only possible contact with them. He needed to speak to them. There might be money owing the family, money for that final job, which had gone so badly wrong. His father, he now saw, was the bombmaker, who had in the end met the same fate which he presumably had dealt out to so many others. His mind churned for a moment, with childhood memories of items seen on the television news: bombs under cars, in trains, in public buildings, people killed, one here, a dozen there, in some cases more than a dozen: the places, Milan, Rome, Verona, Turin, and places abroad, all places where his father surely had been. A list appeared in his mind of all the places his father may have visited for work; and a parallel list, of all the places bombs had gone off; and he imagined for a piercing moment of insight that the two lists coincided perfectly. The police would be working on the lists he was sure, putting things together, reconstructing his father's life, his father's contacts, just as forensic experts were perhaps even now putting his father's blown up body together, seeing if that gave them any clues. How had they identified him? He shuddered at the thought. He felt slightly sick, though just for a moment, but not at the thought of the charred and dismembered body; the nausea was caused not by disgust but by excitement. His father had been, for the most part, at least until the final job, a craftsman. He had been respected and feared. He was his father's son, and he wanted to speak to the people his father had worked for, because he himself wanted to work for them too.

Calogero cautioned his mother not to mention the way of his father's passing, before he called the other children back, and his mother had immediately obeyed his suggestion. She had spent her entire adult life obeying her husband; now the son was the master of the house, and her natural instinct was to defer to him. Assunta and Elena came in, held their mother's hands and wept, because their mother wept. Rosario, twelve years old, looked on puzzled, unsure how to react. The two sons shared a bedroom, and Calogero followed Rosario to their bedroom, where the younger boy sat on his bed and looked up at his elder brother, hoping for guidance, hoping to be told how he should feel, how he should act.

'Was it a car accident?' said Rosario. This was what Calogero had said.

'A very bad one. His body has been badly mangled.'

There was silence between them.

'Will we have enough money?' asked Rosario.

'Yes, plenty. Papa managed things well. He worked hard and he saved and he invested well. And now I will look after things and you will be provided for, and you will not have to worry about anything. The only thing you will have to do is look after mamma and the girls.'

'Me?'

'Yes. Not immediately but soon.'

'Are you going away?'

'Yes, but not far. I will live in one of the other apartments we own. Perhaps even one in this building. I have decided it is time for me to leave home. I will marry Stefania.'

Rosario nodded.

'Now I am going out, and I will be back late. Just in case mamma asks. Tomorrow I will go to the lawyer. You can go to the Church and speak to don Giorgio. We have to organise the funeral.' He thought for a moment of what was left of the body. 'You like don Giorgio, so I leave that to you, and get don Giorgio to come and see mamma. Mamma will expect it. Don't bother going to school tomorrow and tell the girls the same thing. Stay at home. I will see you tomorrow. Now I must get some clean clothes.'

He packed some clothes into a rucksack, put on a baseball cap which Rosario had never seen him wear before now, and then left the house.

Dusk was falling as he reached the street, and he walked quickly to the Via Etnea and turned left. When he reached the Cathedral square, he turned right into the Via Vittorio Emanuele. It only took him a few minutes to reach the shop, which he had last visited a couple of years previously with his father. It had not changed much, and there was the sad depressed figure of signor Vitale in the lit interior, at his counter. He walked in, the door had a bell that clanged, and Vitale looked up. The expression in his eyes betrayed the realisation that he had been expecting a caller, and that the caller was unwelcome.

Calogero stood before the man but did not announce himself. He knew that the man had guessed who he was. He waited for him to speak. At length he did.

'My condolences,' he said. 'I knew your father for many years. For me, he was a good man, a friend. Many people relied on him. He would always be first choice when they had something that needed not strength, though he had that, but finesse, cleverness, subtlety. He had a steady hand. He didn't make mistakes – until now. Perhaps he was losing his touch. The work was delicate. Perhaps he just made one mistake he ought to have avoided. Perhaps he was unlucky. You may not have heard the details. He was in a hotel room near Milan station. The accident made quite a mess. There were police everywhere, or so they tell me. The people he was working for cannot be happy. The whole thing draws unwelcome attention to them, just when they were hoping to not have attention paid to them. The job he was doing was calculated to create silence, to create discretion; the accident he had created, in every sense, a big noise. Now there's an investigation, people asking questions. It will be most unwelcome to those who like nothing better than to be able to get on with their work in peace and quiet. Have the police come to you yet?'

'They came this afternoon, less than two hours ago. They found out nothing. I was not there. My family had nothing to tell them.'

'Of course, of course.'

'I would never speak to them.'

'But you may tell them some things without meaning to,' said Vitale. 'I mean, by coming here. They could follow you, and then draw conclusions. The very first place you came to after their visit....'

'That is why I came at once. If they were to follow me, being the idiots they are, they would put a tail on me tomorrow morning, not tonight. The two who came need to report back, write it up, evaluate, consult, and only after all that would they take action. Tomorrow morning by the very earliest. That is why I came to see you now. Tomorrow would be too risky. I want to see the people who employed my father.'

'Why? You want revenge?' asked the man, astonished.

'No, of course not. It was an accident. I do not hold anyone responsible. I want to meet them and to talk to them.'

'They are not the sort of people who grant meetings to people who request them. If they want to see you, they know where to find you. But why would they want to see you? What have you got for them? Why would they want to meet you? In fact, quite the opposite. Your father, may he rest in peace, made a bad mistake, even if it was not his fault, even if he hardly meant to. Think of something else, not them. How old are you?'

'Sixteen.'

'You have other things to think of. Like looking after your mother, and your sisters and little brother.'

Calogero felt the rebuff, but knew that now was not the time to take offence. He might need this man, either now or later.

'Can you tell them you have seen me?' he asked.

'It doesn't work like that,' said Vitale. 'I don't have any means of getting hold of them. They send me messages. I have no way of sending them messages. They use me when they want to do so. I used to supply your father with certain materials he needed, as I am sure you have worked out by now. Legal things that have illegal uses from time to time. They call upon me when they need me. I never call on them. That is part of the bargain, the unspoken contract. There is nothing I can do for you. If they want to get in touch with you, they will.' Vitale sighed. 'Your father had a storeroom in one of the blocks in your quarter. In one of the basements. I don't know where. I don't know if you will be able to find it. The police would like to do so, I am sure.'

Calogero nodded. He noted the warning. There might be all sorts of embarrassing things in his father's cellar. But worse was the prospect of the police going through the cellars of every building in the quarter and finding the Spanish Madonna. He stood back and looked around the shop. He took in the details. He remembered his first visit there, and all the visits of the past. The place never changed. There was a moment of silence.

'Very well,' he said. 'I will look for my father's cellar. It should not be too hard to find. I know where the title deeds to all his properties are kept. Of course, there may be something down there that connects him with you. If there is, I suppose you would want to be told?'

'Of course.'

'I will look tonight. If I find anything, I will come back to you as soon as I do.'

'Wake me up if necessary,' said Vitale. 'I sleep above the shop. If you ring the bell, I will come down.' Vitale was pensive. 'If the police connect me with your father, then the people who employed your father will be, well, not pleased. You would do well to get rid of the evidence.'

Calogero nodded, and then left.

He walked away as quickly as he could, with his eyes studying the pavement, and with the collar of his jacket pulled up as far as it would go. He only paused at the Cathedral square, where he went to one of the public phones to call Stefania. He was brief and to the point. 'Fifteen minutes,' he said.

He was pleased that she was as prompt as he had hoped she would be. He did not have to kick his heels outside the bar on the Via Etnea which was their usual meeting place. She obeyed his summons. She had clearly changed her clothes he noticed, which was good, and had done so expeditiously. He kissed her cheek.

'We will have a drink,' he said, 'then I will take you out to dinner. We will take my car. We will go to Aci Castello. Take your phone, pick whatever restaurant you like, and then call them to say we are coming. Book a table in my name.'

Calogero himself did not have a mobile phone. The girl was delighted. It wasn't often that they did things like this. They had been trailing around with each other since they were both barely fourteen. He had never expressed any great appreciation for her, or even seemed to delight in her company. This idea of dinner in Aci Castello seemed to promise a more exciting time ahead.

They walked to the square in the heart of Purgatory where he kept his car. His entry into the square attracted the notice of the various boys, including Turiddu, all younger than himself, who looked up at him with expectation, hoping he had something for them. But he waved them away and got into the car with Stefania and drove off. He had been driving for well over a year, though he still didn't have a licence; the car was in his father's name.

Drinks followed, and dinner, and with it very desultory conversation. Stefania noticed that he had studied the level of the petrol tank very carefully, as if calculating whether they had enough petrol to get there, even though it was not far, and the tank was nearly full. She noticed too that several times he looked at his watch. But she knew better than to ask him questions. Calogero had money; she found him attractive with his wide apart brown eyes and his close cropped curly brown hair, and his thickset physique. Moreover, she was used to him. That he generally paid her very little attention, even when they were together, was not something that bothered her. At least he paid her the attention that was her due as his girlfriend: he would not tolerate another man looking at her, and she liked his jealousy. She liked too the fact that he was known to be a man of violence, even at the young age of sixteen. Other sixteen-year olds were boys. He gave her lots of money too; he often called at her house to ask where she was, and what she was doing. In that sense she was not neglected.

He seemed quite keen that night to make dinner last almost as long as possible. It was nearly eleven when they left the restaurant.

'Can we go back to your house?' he asked, as they approached the car.

'My parents are there,' she said.

'So what?' he asked. 'We will go to your bedroom and we will be quiet. They won't notice. And if they do, I do not care, and neither should you.'

He had been in the habit of making love to her in her bedroom in the afternoons when both parents were out, and her other siblings were at school. At night time, they had once or twice used the car, which he had claimed he did not like. They had never spent the night together. His words were peremptory, and she knew that if her parents objected, Calogero would explain things to them.

It was nearing midnight when they got back to the quarter, and they let themselves into her building very quietly, without letting the street door slam. They crept up the staircase. She opened the door to the flat as silently as she could, and they slipped into the darkness of the hallway. He had been there many times before, but perhaps the darkness disorientated him. He brushed against the table near the door, and sent the metal object that sat on the table on it flying. There was a deafening crash.

'Oh Jesus,' said Stefania.

A light went on in her parents' room, and a head – belonging to her father – appeared round the door.

'It is past midnight,' he said crossly, then, seeing Calogero, he reined in his anger and withdrew.

They went into her bedroom, aware of the now no longer sleeping parents and other children on the other side of the wall. Stefania had a fit of the giggles as she took her clothes off. He rapidly undressed as well, and they made love without any further ado.

'Too late, too late,' he said, when she tried to make him pause.

Later, he said, as if to answer her objections: 'I want you to get pregnant.'

'Why?' she asked, surprised, worried and a little thrilled by this admission.

'My father is dead,' said Calogero.

He felt her surprise, her shock.

'Car accident, in Milan.'

'I am so sorry,' she said.

She had not known his father, he reflected. How could she be sorry? But that was what one said. It was the expected form of words. She might even have meant it.

'Next year, I will marry you. In the summer. We will both be seventeen. We are grown up enough. Besides, it is good to marry young. Tomorrow I have to see the lawyer and the priest, but I will also come and see your father and mother. Sometime in the early evening. I shall pacify them for making a noise at midnight. I will pacify them for taking their daughter's virginity. How does that sound? My father owns, owned, a nice flat overlooking the square with a view of the Church of the Holy Souls in Purgatory. There are tenants, but I am quite sure they will move out if I ask them to do so. I think we will live there. But you can see it first, and I will give you the money to do it up as you want to. Oh, and I want you to stop thinking about getting a job now you are to be married. Besides, when we are married we will have a baby, I hope.'

She said nothing, but he could feel her excitement. On the other side of the wall he could almost feel her parents' joy as well, if they had been listening. They were the ones who had allowed her to spend all hours with him, only because, well, it was him, he supposed. He would never allow his sisters the same freedom, whoever wanted to take them out, let along his daughters. But Stefania's parents had sensed he was important. Well, that flattered him. And he needed a wife. One might as well take what was offered. He was entering into man's estate.

'I will buy you an engagement ring tomorrow,' he said generously, pleased with the evening's transaction. He had lost a father, gained his adulthood, acquired a wife, all on one night, and the night was not over yet.

Later, much later, he woke her up, getting out of bed, and putting on his clothes.

'I have to go home, as I had better be there in the morning when they wake up,' he whispered. 'And to avoid seeing your father and rubbing his nose in it. Go back to sleep. It is very late. It is three o'clock.'

'Already?' she asked.

He showed her his watch. The dial was luminous. Then he took the rucksack he had brought with him, and left.

Later, at home, suddenly, Rosario woke up. Someone had switched the light on. It was his brother Calogero.

'I knew you would be awake,' he said.

'I wasn't,' said the boy sleepily, screwing up his eyes against the blinding electric light.

'It is three o'clock in the morning,' said Calogero, quickly switching off the light before the boy could check.

'Is it?' said Rosario.

'Of course it is, look, my watch has a luminous dial,' he said, showing it to him. 'Don't worry about anything. Soon you will have this room to yourself. I am marrying Stefania next year.'

'You asked her? She said yes?'

'Don't sound surprised. Of course she did.'

'Why are you wearing different clothes?' Rosario suddenly asked.

'I am not,' said Calogero.

'But you are,' said the younger boy, stubbornly repeating the truth.

Calogero said nothing, but continued to change into his sleeping clothes. Only after he had done this, he approached his brother's bed, with great deliberation, and pulled him up by the hair into an upright position.

'What did you say?' he asked, his voice a whisper.

Rosario knew he had made a mistake, and he knew that it was too late to correct it. His brother was now holding him by the ear, which was painful. He knew what was coming. But even the terrible fear of punishment had at this moment to coexist with a distraction. There was a smell of petrol in the room.

'Shut up and go to sleep,' whispered Calogero, holding his brother's ear in a tight and painful embrace. 'You are not going to school tomorrow, remember. I am tired right now, but tomorrow I will have more energy and you will receive the full force of my belt. You never learn, do you?'

Calogero released his ear, went to his own bed, and was presently asleep. Rosario, now awake, heard his calm breathing as he lay miserably in the dark.

The nickname 'The Chemist' was an invention of the newspapers, or at least some imaginative journalist working for a paper, no one ever could remember which or whom. But Calogero's father, Renato di Rienzi, soon became known by this name and this name alone. Once the investigation began, and the newspapers and television publicized it, the public, ever hungry for such tales, was entertained and frightened by the story of the man who had briefly been a science teacher with a particular aptitude for chemistry (so one retired long lost colleague claimed to remember) and who had then gone on to be the expert at assassination through bombmaking, until fate had caught up with him, and he had died in the same way as his many victims.

As for his supplier, Vitale, who had kept the hardware shop in Via Vittorio Emanuele, and who had died the very day after the Chemist met his end, thanks to the conflagration that had engulfed his shop in the middle of the night, the public was able to connect the two events, when directed to do so by the papers and television. The media in this were quicker than the police, who had not seen any connection and had kept the two investigations separate. But the journalists saw the obvious link. The Chemist had blown himself up because the supplier had supplied him with either the wrong things or with faulty goods. The details underpinning this story were never supplied, but the legend was born that the employers of the Chemist, outraged by the loss of their trusted man, their premier operative, the man they had relied on for the spectacular disposal of their enemies, had killed his supplier out of pique and rage, and as a warning to others. Naturally the men behind the supplier, the men who really counted, wanted to hide their tracks, and thus had decided to get rid of Vitale, lest he lead the police to them. At least that was a common supposition.

Of course, there could be even more to it than met the eye, and there were many who were quick to credit the theory that the supplier had been working for the police, wittingly or unwittingly, and the whole thing, beginning with the bomb that went wrong, was something set up by the police to make the Chemist's employers look stupid, something, everyone agreed, they very much disliked.

And why had the Chemist been in Milan in the first place? Who had he been sent to blow up? Was Milan indeed his final destination, or was he just preparing the bomb there, in order to transport it to another place for detonation? As it turned out, several fairly important people were in Milan on the day of the explosion, or due to visit within the next few days. (It was pointed out that this was the case any day of the year, given the importance of Milan, but this was dismissed by those who loved a good conspiracy theory). Numerous names were suggested as the intended target: the newly appointed Prime Minister, Silvio Berlusconi himself, or the Minister of Foreign Affairs, several members of parliament, the president of the Council of Europe, the list was long; perhaps even the managers of the Milan underground railway, who were the centre of another scandal. For the more you went into it, the more conspiracies emerged, conspiracies that seemed to connect and join up and unite as one huge overarching plot.

Certainly every unsolved murder in the last two decades might have had something to do with the Chemist and his associates. The Chemist, in death, assumed monstrous proportions. In death he became famous, whereas in life, he had been unknown.

The neighbours were sorry for Maria, Calogero's mother, and for her daughters, Assunta and Elena. They were good people, and obviously the signora had had no idea whatever that her husband had been a bad man. To her he had just been her husband. They had married when she was eighteen and spent twenty happy years together. She had not questioned. Her daughters neither. She had not known. She had chosen not to know, to stay on the path of ignorance. She was determined not to know, not even now, not ever. In her mind she shut it all out. Yet she resolved to devote herself to praying for his soul, praying that God would overlook the Chemist's sins. But in her presence the matter was never discussed. She was insulated by an envelope of silence and denial. When don Giorgio, the priest from the Church of the Holy Souls in Purgatory, came to see her and condole with her, she acted as if she were just any grieving woman who had lost her husband.

As for Calogero, on whom the mantle of adulthood had suddenly fallen, no one discussed it with him either, and he too was surrounded by silence on this matter. But it was acknowledged. When he went to the square outside the church, the open space in which he had grown up, where the boys of the Purgatory quarter hung out, he was acknowledged as the supreme leader, not just by the younger ones, whom he had always dominated, but by his contemporaries as well. He was now the son of the Chemist, the eldest son of one of Sicily's most notorious paid killers, against whom, of course, nothing had been proven in a court of law, and who might, after all, have been the victim of some police plot. He was the son not quite of a hero, but the son of someone. And he was feared. But he had always been feared.

As for the supplier in the Via Vittorio Emanuele hardware shop, Vitale, the theories about his death could be summed up as follows. Perhaps he had in chagrin set fire to his own shop, in an attempt to collect the insurance money, and accidentally been overcome by fumes. Perhaps the employers of the Chemist had killed him. But perhaps too Calogero had killed him. The exact cause of his death was hard to determine, given that all that was left of him were his charred remains, and that the shop had contained so many different chemical substances that it had created a merry forensic hell.

And what were the investigators thinking? How were their minds working? Almost three months after the events in the Via Vittorio

Emanuele, the police working on the case made the perhaps ill-judged decision to call in the Chemist's elder son for questioning.

Calogero came voluntarily. It was a few days before Christmas. He had a lawyer with him, a man whom his father had employed to help with the contracts to do with the properties, a man who assured Calogero that he knew nothing about crime. Calogero assured him he did not need to do so, and that his presence would be purely ornamental.

He was interviewed by the two policemen who had come to the flat that day to give them the news of his father's death. They pretended, or so it seemed to him, that they had asked him in to let him know about how the enquiry was going. They affected that air of ease that falls on all working people in the last few days before the Christmas holiday. But he was not fooled.

The older one, a man nearing retirement called Storace, spoke about the bomb that had killed his father. Their forensic experts had traced various things that they had found in that hotel room by Milan station to Vitale's shop. But once more Calogero was not fooled. He had seen the report on the television. There cannot have been any forensic evidence worth having, as far as he could see, the destruction being so total. It had been a huge bomb and had brought down half the hotel. At the funeral the coffin had been empty, as he knew, though the rest of the family did not. This talk of forensic evidence was a fishing expedition.

Did he know signor Vitale? Had he known his father had known him and called at his shop relatively often? Had he been to Vitale's shop with his father? Or on his own?

No, no, no, he answered laconically to each question. And he knew that they had no proof at all. No one had seen him there, or at least no one remembered seeing him there.

'Your father owned a lot of properties in the Purgatory quarter,' then said the younger one, a man not more than twenty-five years old, who was called Volta.

'Yes, he did,' answered Calogero. 'I thought you might ask about them, and want to examine them perhaps, so I asked signor Rossi for a list. Here it is. It is complete.'

The lawyer Rossi handed over the list, looking deeply uncomfortable. Of course the list was not complete; one property had been left off, and the police would soon discover which because they would have their own list from the land registry and would rush to visit the one property they thought he was hiding, a storeroom under a block of flats in the quarter, which had been the Chemist's laboratory, and which Calogero was glad for them to see. Rossi had been made party to this deception a moment before the interview began.

'Where were you the night signor Vitale died?' Storace now asked.

Died, not murdered, noted Calogero, leaving the face-saving idea that he had died in an accident.

'It was the night we came to tell your mother about your father's death. You will remember,' said Volta.

'I certainly do,' said Calogero. 'How can I forget it? That night I went for drinks with my girlfriend Stefania, and then we went to have dinner in a restaurant in Aci Castello – the name escapes me – but I am sure I could take you there. She booked the table. It was a long dinner. Then I took Stefania home, and we arrived at her place at midnight. Her parents were up – well not quite: we woke them up when we got in. Then I went to bed with my girlfriend, and then I left her at three in the morning, and went home to my place, and went to bed in the room I share with my brother. And stayed there till morning.'

'And they will remember all this?' asked Volta with a touch of irony.

'I am sure they will. The people in the restaurant will know us, I am sure. That night I got engaged to Stefania and that night I made her pregnant. You ask her. She will not have forgotten either event. Right now she is near enough three months gone. It was a nice surprise. No one outside the family knows yet. Just you. We are getting married in the summer. Then when I went home, my little brother Rosario was already in bed, and still awake, so I did my best to comfort him as he was so upset. Like me, he won't have forgotten. And he won't have forgotten the time, because I told him it was so late, and showed him the time on my watch. The dial is luminous.'

'You do not have a phone, a mobile?' asked Volta, curiously.

'I do not like them,' said Calogero. 'I like being free. I do not like being at everyone's beck and call all day long.'

'What clothes were you wearing that night?' asked the older policeman, Storace.

'Normal clothes,' said Calogero. 'Just as I am wearing now.'

'You still have them?'

'Yes. In fact I think I was wearing the jeans I am wearing now. They are my second best pair. I have not thrown any of my clothes away since then, as far as I can remember.'

'And you had a rucksack with you that evening? And one of those hats, what do you call them, that all young people wear?' asked Storace.

'A baseball cap?' said Volta.

'No,' said Calogero. 'I never wear hats. They are very old-fashioned. Even my father didn't wear a hat. And for the type I think you mean, the ones the Americans wear, no, I have never possessed one.'

'And the rucksack?' said Volta.

'I have several at home. They are very useful. Women have handbags and men have rucksacks. But that evening I did not have a rucksack. I usually would have done, but not that evening.'

'You are sure?'

'Positive.'

'How can you be so sure?'

'Because there was a point that night when I went to get something from my rucksack and realised that I had left the rucksack behind; my father had just died, and I was not thinking straight. That is how my girlfriend got pregnant. I forgot the rucksack.'

'Your girlfriend's parents let you sleep with her in the house?'

'They do now. We are getting married.'

'Congratulations. You are young to marry.'

'I am an adult.'

'We can see that.'

With a weary sigh, they wished him a happy Christmas and let him go. The next day they did make some progress in their investigation, though: they uncovered the storeroom in the basement of one of the buildings in the Purgatory quarter. This was opened to great fanfare on the television, where it was treated as great a discovery as Tutankhamun's tomb. The police claimed huge credit for the discovery of the Chemist's secret laboratory, oblivious to the fact that Calogero had thrown them this sop, in order to stop them finding the Spanish Madonna, hidden in another storeroom in another block of flats. The discovery of the laboratory gave them one thing for sure, apart from a publicity coup and the completely false impression that progress was being made. It established a clear link between the Chemist and Vitale, as much of the stuff stored there could be traced back to Vitale's burned out shop.

But were they any further on? It was clear to them that the burning out of Vitale's shop could not possibly be a coincidence, and the fact that it happened the night the news of the Chemist's death arrived in Catania had to be significant. Moreover, they knew that someone in a baseball cap and carrying a rucksack had been seen in the vicinity of the shop at 2am. There was camera footage to prove it. The trouble was that the camera footage was very grainy and provided no clear picture of the person's face; nor was the camera footage actually close to the shop; it was very unlikely to make any impression in court. But both Storace and Volta thought that the man in the hat was either Calogero or someone sent by the Chemist's employers, or that the former and the latter were the same person. Unless of course it was a complete red herring; but it was all they had to go on for the present.

In order to investigate the alibi further, they hit upon another line of investigation. It would be completely pointless to interview the pregnant girlfriend, who would say whatever Calogero wanted her to say. But they could speak to the younger boy. The elder boy was clearly a thug and a brute, a hard nut to crack, and clever with it, but their intelligence suggested that the younger boy was completely different in character, softer, more pliable, more likely to cooperate, more likely to give something away without realising it, more likely to crack under questioning, and of course only twelve years old. They picked him up one afternoon at the school gates, in the beginning of January, when the school holidays were over.

There are certain rules and regulations about the questioning of minors in Italy, as in other countries, and these have to be observed if anything is going to be used as evidence later. So, Rosario was taken to a room with soft furnishings where a kind lady was present to ensure fair play, and there put to the question. They kept him for as long as they could, perhaps longer, and then released him, so he came home to a late supper.

The boy ate in front of his mother, who did not ask where he had been. In her presence, Calogero was equally silent. It was only after supper, when Rosario took his school bag from the kitchen floor to the bedroom the brothers shared, that he and Calogero were alone and able to speak.

'I didn't make a fuss, I didn't call the lawyer,' said Calogero. 'I thought that if I did that, they would think we had something to hide. You know nothing, I know nothing. There is nothing to tell. And they let you go; so I suppose they now see that there is nothing to tell too.'

Rosario was mute and miserable. Calogero waited for him to speak. At last, with great difficulty, Rosario spoke.

'How did you know where I was?' he asked.

'One of the boys at your school saw you go with them and knew I would want to know.' He waited. 'So what happened?'

'They told me... they showed me a list. A list of all the people they say Papa murdered. Thirty or forty of them, at least, and another hundred or so probable victims. What he did was wrong.'

Calogero was expressionless.

'Strangers talk badly of your father, and you believe them? What proof have they got? These people are born liars. You must never talk like this about your father again. Do you understand me? He is your father. They are strangers. Whatever your father did, he did it for you. You are so ungrateful.'

Rosario looked at his brother defiantly.

'What he did was wrong,' he repeated, barely being able to repeat the words, knowing what was coming.

'You need educating,' said Calogero.

He grabbed his brother by the hair and pulled him to his feet; then he kicked him sharply in the shins, at which he fell to the floor. Then going to a drawer, he extracted a belt which he used to beat the boy, slowly and methodically.

Two rooms away, the mother of the boy heard her elder son beat her younger, and heard Rosario's sobs and groans. She turned up the sound on the television, and continued stonily to watch the news, while silent tears formed in her eyes. Later, Calogero appeared, and sat next to her and drank a glass of water. Neither spoke. Rosario kept to his room.

What Calogero did not know then, but knew later, when the story emerged, for at least one of the police, either Storace or Volta, or the sympathetic lady, talked about it, was the substance of the interview between Rosario and the police. They had questioned him closely about his brother's movements on the night of the death of Vitale. In particular they had wanted to know when Calogero had come home. Rosario had answered that he had come home at three in the morning. Moreover, he said he knew that it was the correct night because his brother had told him he was getting married. He had remembered the date, the day they had told him of his father's death. And he had looked at the clock. He was, when questioned time and again, adamant on this point; he had looked at the clock. It had said three. His brother had not left again that night.

He was asked about his brother's luminous watch, time and again, and each time he gave what he was sure was the answer Calogero wanted: he had seen it was three in the morning on the clock next to his bed, not on the luminous watch face. Then the direction of the questions had changed. What had his brother been wearing? In particular, when he came in at three in the morning, was he wearing the same clothes he had left the house in earlier? Or was he wearing different clothes? Was he wearing a baseball cap? Was he carrying a rucksack?

Rosario had known immediately that the answer to these questions was vital. But he did not know what the answer he should give should be at first. His brother had changed clothes, he had remembered that at the time, because he thought it unusual; and he had put a spare set of clothes into the rucksack before he had left, and not come back with the rucksack. He thought quickly. He answered that he had not noticed anything special about his brother's appearance at all that evening. As for the rucksack, he didn't think so, but he could not be sure. He often carried a rucksack, but not always. He looked at the two policemen, to see if this was the answer they had hoped for. They looked exasperated. It wasn't the answer they wanted, clearly.

He was asked what his brother carried in his rucksack. Here Rosario was on surer ground. He knew that Caloriu always carried a knife in the rucksack, and that this was something he needed to deny. He maintained that he had never seen his brother put anything in his rucksack or take anything out of it.

The police sighed once more. It was, naturally enough, a lie, but it was a lie that was convincingly and unhesitatingly told. He explained that his brother was very possessive about his rucksack.

He had, he realised, done his best to protect his brother, but his brother had punished him all the same. He was not sure if he wanted his brother's approval. As he cried in his bed that evening, what had hurt him more, the beating he had received? The humiliation of it? Or was it the fact that while he had refused to deny the truth about his father, a killer, he had not had the courage to admit the truth about his brother, now getting away with his first murder? His brother who had smelt of the petrol he had used to burn out the shop in the Via Vittoria Emanuele.

The police interview with Rosario, when its details were known, had another effect. It introduced into popular lore the idea that the police had suspected Calogero, but failed to prove it. Calogero was sixteen, and could kill with impunity. But no one knew this for sure. Only as time passed did Rosario come to reconstruct what must have happened. The false alibi was easy enough. Between three and four in the morning, with a rucksack containing new clothes and some petrol siphoned off from the car, and a knife, Calogero had gone to Vitale's, who had let him in, whereupon Calogero had knifed the man, doused the shop in petrol, abandoned his knife and his clothes in the fire, and then walked home in the spare set of clothes. The shop had been full of combustibles, he had seen in the news, and that had covered up the crime.

Could it be so? Others seemed to have no difficulty attributing such ruthlessness to Calogero; nothing was said, everything was assumed. As for Rosario, the way his brother had smelt of petrol, and had made him smell of petrol too, this lingered in the memory.

Chapter Three

Calogero married Stefania just a few days after his seventeenth birthday. It was the month of May, and she was seven months pregnant. The ceremony was celebrated in the Church of the Holy Souls in Purgatory, where, back in late October, his father's funeral Mass had taken place with its suspiciously light coffin; the celebrant on both occasions was don Giorgio, the priest in charge of the Church.

Don Giorgio was a man and a priest of very pronounced judgements, and he was not good at hiding what he felt, which had rather held back his career in the Church. At the age of fifty-five he was not even a parish priest, merely in the employ of the Confraternity of the Holy Souls in Purgatory, which paid him a reasonable stipend and gave him a place to live next to the Church. Don Giorgio had been shocked by the revelations about the Chemist, and how the man, whom he had barely known, and who had never attracted much attention to himself, had been Italy's most accomplished mass murderer of the decade. He had been shocked and angered. The man had been living in the quarter, in plain sight, doing his deadly work for years and years, and no one had known anything or seen anything; and it was worse than that. When his villainy was revealed, when the man was blown up with his own bomb, he had become a figure of legend, a folk hero. No one had condemned him or scorned his memory. Of course don Giorgio had done his funeral; his widow was a good woman and his younger son was a good boy and a fine altar server; but he had expected the funeral to be a very low key affair, a matter of prayer and penance for a soul who if not in hell, would spend a very long time in purgatory. But that was not how things had turned out. The Mass had been sparsely attended, with just the family present and some of the women of the quarter, who, pious souls, always went to funerals to pray for the departed. But when the coffin had left the church, the entire square had been milling with people, people from the quarter, and people from all over Catania as far as he could judge, and numerous police and even, what a disgrace, a camera crew from RAI. And the bad elements had, on seeing the cameras, knowing that they would be on the news that very night, provided the show the whole of Italy craved: they had applauded a criminal. They had shouted out words of praise to the Chemist's corpse; they had acclaimed the Chemist's son. And the whole of Italy had seen it later that day on the television news. The people of Purgatory, criminals themselves, saying farewell to one of their own. And the smiling face of Calogero was there for the whole nation to see.

Worse was to come. The Vicar-General of the diocese (who dealt with matters of clergy discipline) summoned don Giorgio for a dressing down. This was a very painful occasion, for don Giorgio was reminded that the Archdiocese of Catania, like the rest of the Church, had a very strict policy about not granting showy funerals to criminals, and not letting criminal organisations use the Church to glorify themselves. The funeral of the Chemist had degenerated into a display of the very worst type. Don Giorgio felt he had to defend himself, and in so doing he found that he was defending Calogero, which was very much going against the grain. He pointed out that the Chemist was not strictly speaking a criminal, and had never been convicted of any crime. Moreover, his son Calogero was not convicted of any crime either, and thus not a criminal. In making these arguments, he realised he was standing on very shaky ground, exactly the sort of territory on which he would never normally have chosen to fight.

The Vicar General held up a pitying hand, to stop him.

'Do you honestly believe that these men are or were innocent? Do such crowds turn out for the funerals of innocent wronged men?'

Indeed they both knew the innocent and wronged were buried without fanfare, particularly in Sicily.

'The demonstration, which was most unsavoury, all took place outside the Church. What happened inside was very ordinary. The RAI cameras were there, outside. I would not have dreamed of letting them in,' said don Giorgio.

'I sympathise with your difficulty,' said the Vicar General, who was not a bad man. 'I will point this out to the Archbishop. The people who behave badly in these circumstances are those who never go to Mass; and there are plenty of those about. As for the people of your quarter, they are the very worst. I am afraid that is not your fault. I am sure you have done your best to convert them. But even Saint Charles Borromeo would fail with that lot. But the truth is that the Archbishop made me call you in, because he got a phone call from the Cardinal in Palermo, who felt the television pictures made him look bad; and the Cardinal would only have phoned because someone higher up phoned him.'

'Someone in the Vatican?'

'I imagine so. They are very touchy about the way we are seen, the way the Church is seen, the way Sicily is seen. The Church and criminality going together – it's a gift to the anti-clericals, to the Protestants, to the Anglo-Saxons. But we live with the reality and we know it is not true. The Church has nothing to do with crime.'

As soon as he said this, the realisation hung between them that this was not entirely true. They had nothing to do with crime as such; but they lived in a crime ridden society, and the criminals were everywhere, and there was no avoiding them.

'What is this Calogero like?' asked the Vicar General.

'He is depraved. His father was a cold-blooded professional killer. I imagine he has inherited the parental gene. But his mother is a good woman, his sisters are innocent, and his younger brother is my altar server, and a very good boy.'

'The wheat and the tares often grow in the same field, as the Lord Himself pointed out,' said the Vicar General. 'I will pacify the Archbishop. Indeed, I imagine that he is already pacified. He knows that the Cardinal in Palermo, and the people in Rome even more so, simply do not understand.'

Don Giorgio, after this conversation, conceived a loathing for Calogero, who summed up for him everything that was bad about the people of the quarter. The man had spent his childhood and early teenage years as a petty thief (everyone knew that), he never went to Mass, and he had perhaps murdered this man Vitale, and outwitted the police. And yet, when Calogero came to see him with Stefania, wanting to get married, just after the funeral, he felt he could not refuse. There was the man's mother to think of, and there was Rosario to think of too. If he were to make difficulties, the younger boy might suffer. So he agreed. The wedding Mass would take place in Purgatory, and the reception would happen in a grand hotel in Acitrezza; and he knew that few would attend the Mass, and the vulgar display would take place well away from the Church and the quarter.

As it turned out he did get to witness the vulgar display at the wedding reception, because he was invited to it, and in his curiosity he could not stay away. Given that his father had been such a silent and invisible type, he was amazed that Calogero's guest list was so extensive. Of course, there were the bride's guests to consider as well, but it seemed that most of the quarter was there, and many other people besides. The whole thing disgusted the priest. The bride was wearing the most overdone of dresses, and looked like a Christmas tree; the groom was wearing a shiny new suit, and was receiving huge attention. The tables groaned with food and the drink flowed without stint. It must have cost a huge amount: but the Chemist had been rich and never spent much; and Calogero had been stealing wallets for years. Don Giorgio was mesmerised by the sight of people queuing to congratulate Calogero, handing him envelopes stuffed with cash, and touching him, as if for good luck. He had entered into man's estate, indeed, and was blessed by the gods.

Standing a little apart, with a beer in his hand, the priest felt cut off from this alien scene. He felt the eyes of many on him, felt their hostility and disapproval. They knew that he knew, and they did not like it. But that was the price one paid, if one lived in Purgatory. He was a little surprised and also a little pleased, to find Anna the Romanian prostitute standing next to him. Her little boy, whose First Holy Communion was that very week, wanted to say hello to the priest, she explained, as if to excuse her own presence. The child, sweet and dark haired, spoke to the priest, seeking confirmation of the promise that he would be able to become an altar boy once he had done his First Holy Communion. This, it seemed was his one great ambition. Don Giorgio then turned to the mother. She, unlike some, never missed Mass, and the boy always accompanied her. Of course, he knew her profession, and he regretted it, and she perhaps did too, he sensed. He had the impression that she shared his dislike of Calogero. But this was the world they lived in, and there was no other world.

Shortly afterwards, still clutching his glass of Peroni, he found that a small depressed looking man was standing next to him.

'Who was she, Father?' he asked.

'That is Anna, one of the women of the quarter, she is originally from Romania,' he replied.

'A beautiful woman,' remarked the man, without any hint of lechery.

'Yes.'

He realised that he was talking to the lawyer Rossi, one of the six hundred or so members of the Confraternity of the Holy Souls in Purgatory. He barely knew the lawyer Rossi, but it was always wise to keep the members of the Confraternity happy; he realised that Rossi, who seemed crushed by the experience of the wedding, as if to show that these were not his sort of people at all, and that he was only here under duress, was a little bit drunk.

'Why are you here?' asked the priest.

'I am his lawyer,' said Rossi. 'God help me. I was his father's lawyer. I had no idea. I just handled the contracts for him, you know, with the tenants. That is what I do. I work for Petrocchi.'

Don Giorgio saw how things fitted together. The lawyer Petrocchi was the head of a big law firm; this Rossi was one of his very minor understrappers; Petrocchi was the head of the Confraternity, the man whom don Giorgio dealt with when it came to the restoration of the Church and his own personal stipend, not to mention his pension contributions.

'I never knew,' said Rossi, 'I never realised that the Chemist, as they now call him, was anything more than a normal slum landlord. I knew one should not look too closely. But it was Petrocchi who put the work my way. He told me it would all be very simple. And it was. Then the man died – and you know how that happened – after all you did the funeral, I was there. Then the complications started.' Don Giorgio nodded, hoping the lawyer would go on. He did go on. 'I had to accompany him to the police when they questioned him. The police are sure he was responsible for the death of Vitale. That he stabbed him, and then burned down his shop to cover up the crime. That he manufactured an alibi using the girlfriend, now the wife, and the little brother. I sat through the interrogation, and I knew what they were getting at. The questions – it was clear what they were about. He went to see Vitale in the middle of the night, no doubt on some urgent business, and he was carrying a rucksack with a change of clothes. When you stab someone, there is always blood, and you have to get rid of your clothes and put on new ones. Everyone knows that. He lied about having the rucksack. He got the small boy to lie as well. As a result, they cannot touch him; they cannot prove even that Vitale was murdered. But everyone knows it.'

'But why would he want to kill Vitale?'

Rossi laughed. 'Because you are no one until you have killed someone. Once you do that you become a leader. And it is the best way of advertising your services to the friends in Palermo.'

Rossi, the priest saw, was more drunk than he had at first assumed.

'The work I have had to do. You would not believe. The Confraternity has put the widow on the list.' Don Giorgio knew what this meant. The list was a group of charitable benefactions to widows and orphans. 'Five hundred euro a month, for life. Not bad, eh?'

'That is generous. The signora is a good woman, and the other children are good too.'

'Even if their father wasn't.'

'Even if their father wasn't,' echoed the priest.

'Petrocchi did that. I was left to handle the will. I could go to jail for twenty years, God help me.'

'Why?'

'There was no will. What we got proved in court was a forgery. God help us all. I know it was wrong. But Calogero is not the sort of man to whom you can say no. The will left everything to him, and left the rest of them as his dependants. Well, there is plenty of money. As long as he is generous, they will be fine. And they have the 500 a month from the Confraternity. As for all this extravagance,' said Rossi, practically spitting out the word in a mixture of jealousy and contempt, 'all this expense, do you think this costs him anything? Do you think the people who own this hotel will dare to send him a bill, or a proper bill that reflects what this costs? They will write it off as a useful loss. Same with the people who have done up his flat. He is not the sort of man you dare invoice. Do you think I have done so? Huh. I work for free. More fool me, more fool all of us. I wish to God I had left Sicily when I was younger, before it was too late. Now it is too late. I am stuck.'

Rossi shambled off. Don Giorgio was left alone with his Peroni. He found the whole thing most oppressive. There was the girl, showing off to her friends, who were admiring her rings and her wedding dress; she was lifting it slightly so they could see the shoes. Shoes! He felt a wave of contempt. There were the girl's parents, pleased to have married her off at the age of seventeen to a rich thug. There was the groom in his shiny blue suit, and his dark red tie, his wide apart brown eyes looking at everyone in the room, as if checking on their behaviour, people standing before him, demanding his attention, stroking his arm, looking at his face lovingly, as if he were some god come down to earth, some lucky token, some guarantee from heaven to protect them from the cruelty of life.

He left the room, preparing to go home. Outside the hotel the carpark was full of cars and small boys of various ages, all in their suits, admiring the various vehicles. He recognised them from the square outside the Church. How boring their lives were. Most did not seem to go to school, but spent their days hanging around. That was what they were doing now, looking at the cars, some with approval, others not. And there, sitting on the steps was Rosario, not with the other boys, but looking on curiously.

The priest sat down next to the child, and asked him if he were enjoying himself. The boy shook his head. Don Giorgio had long known that Rosario was not happy. The child seemed permanently depressed. It was not hard to see why. But surely things would now get better, as Calogero and his bride moved into their new flat in the square which would have, he reflected, a beautiful view of the Church of the Holy Souls in Purgatory. They had been very lucky in the way the previous tenants had relinquished it so quickly and without fuss. And the whole place had been refurbished - another huge expenditure. Calogero, he saw, was very keen to announce he was rich.

Then suddenly Calogero was there, on the other side of Rosario, sitting on the step. The atmosphere changed. He could sense Rosario stiffen. Calogero did not look at his brother, but looked over him to don Giorgio.

'Father,' he said, with a charming smile. 'You have been so kind. Everyone was saying how beautiful the Mass was, and how lovely the Church was looking, and how lucky we were to have Rosario as an altar server. I am truly grateful.' He took out an envelope from his shiny blue jacket pocket and handed it to the priest, who had no choice but to take it. 'I have been meaning to give you this. It is for you,' he added redundantly. 'A sign of my gratitude, and Stefania's too. As you know, I am a bad Catholic and a bad man' – he smiled winningly – 'but I have to say God has been good to me, despite the recent misfortune and the loss of my father. And you know in a few months' time, there is no point hiding it any longer, we will have a baptism, in your Church of course, with you officiating. It is a great blessing. I cannot quite believe it.' The boys from the carpark, at the appearance of their hero, had now gathered round. One, the one called Turiddu, sat next to Calogero but on a lower step and looked up at him as he spoke. The others stood around. 'It was of course not intended,' continued Calogero. 'We always wanted to marry, but we also wanted to wait. But that night, the night we heard my father was dead, we were both so upset, that we broke all the rules for the first time, and God rewarded us like this, a child and a marriage resulting.'

The expression on the other boys' faces was a mixture of puzzlement, pride and admiration. The god had procreated at the first attempt. It was nothing short of a miracle. Don Giorgio was embarrassed and disgusted. He wished once more that he had refused to do the wedding. He wished he could hand back the envelope he had just received. He noticed a curious thing. The boy they called Turiddu, who was the same age as Rosario, thirteen, was leaning his arm on Calogero's knee, and Calogero was lightly holding his hand. Calogero was looking at don Giorgio defiantly.

The little group broke up; but don Giorgio remained on the step, as did Rosario, and as did Turiddu. Turiddu stared at the priest, taking the hint from his master, who, despite his kind words, clearly saw the priest as an enemy. Indeed, Turiddu knew that Calogero had made a fool of the priest numerous times. He had stolen the Spanish Madonna that now lay in what had been Turiddu's father's storeroom, the very Madonna that don Giorgio was supposed to look after and protect; he had been the centre of attention at the Chemist's funeral, essentially upstaging the Church itself; and he had lived an immoral life, stealing wallets and car radios, the sort of life that supposedly earned you eternal damnation, but which for the moment only brought great reward. Who cared about eternal life, when the here and now was so enjoyable? Why worry about hell, when there was a world like this to enjoy, and men like don Giorgio to humiliate and anger?

Don Giorgio looked at Turiddu and took in his details. He knew the boy, and had baptised him, and taught him his catechism for Holy Communion. He looked at the way he was wearing a shiny blue suit like his idol. He looked at his upper lip, covered by the lightest of down, and the few spots on his chin, his dirty blond hair and his light blue eyes: so young and so depraved, the very picture of evil. He could sense that Rosario strongly disliked the boy, but also feared him. The fear was everywhere. The whole Purgatory quarter lived in fear. He himself was not afraid, but he was afraid for Rosario.

'I am going back home,' he said, realising that Turiddu was not going to leave. 'I will take a taxi. Rosario, do you want to go back home too?'

Rosario shook his head once more. 'I have to stay here until midnight at least,' he said.

Don Giorgio left, knowing that he would have to speak to Rosario, but not now. But the time would come. He wandered across the hotel car park in the heat of the evening. Dusk had come. Behind him he could hear the diminishing sound of the celebrations. Standing at the entrance to the car park was a young man in a suit, who looked at him intently. He did not recognise him, and he was sure he had not seen him before, either in church or in the hotel. He stopped, sensing that the man wished to speak to him.

'Good evening, don Giorgio,' said the man.

'Good evening,' replied don Giorgio.

The man, now he had caught his attention and aroused his curiosity, had stepped back in to the gathering shadows, as if he did not want to be seen by anyone else, or recognised by any of the wedding guests.

'My name is Volta,' said the man. 'I am a policeman.'

'Are you on duty?' asked don Giorgio.

'No, I am here in a personal capacity. I came because I wanted to see who else would be here. I wanted to get a feel for the people Calogero di Rienzi hangs out with. I take an interest.'

'So do I. I came because I was curious too,' confessed don Giorgio. 'Have you found anything out?'

'Not really. Your Calogero is clever. But one day he will make a mistake, you'll see. But he has a long way to go before that happens, I think. It will be an interesting tale. I am keen to follow it every step of the way.'

'So, you are not working on his case?'

'There is no case,' said Volta. 'I am here purely to indulge my curiosity.'

'You are young,' said don Giorgio. 'You may live to see the end of the story, unlike some of the rest of us.'

He passed on, looking for his taxi.

The newly married couple went on honeymoon to a very expensive hotel in Taormina. Stefania had wanted to go a little bit further away, specifically to Rome, or perhaps Florence; neither she nor Calogero had ever been 'abroad', that is, on the other side of the straits of Messina. This was the subject of their first disagreement. He wanted to go to Rome as well, very much, but now was not the time, given her condition, and besides, he had a fixed idea of what honeymoons entailed, and thought that the business of honeymooning would distract them from the matter of sightseeing. Underneath this, she could see, were their differing attitudes to their own provincialism, the way they dealt with the matter of their origins. While in Taormina, she sensed his dislike of the people they saw who were evidently from the north of Italy, as one could tell by their accent, their dress, the way they looked, the way they walked. But if he disliked them, as indeed did she, she wanted to emulate them. She had already started lightening her hair, creeping gradually towards that blessed state of blondeness to which perhaps every Sicilian woman aspired. She studied their clothes and their shoes, above all their shoes; she looked at the men, and saw what they wore, and made note of the clothes she would buy for her husband. Already she sensed that her own wedding dress, and the suit he had worn at the wedding, had not been quite right.

The hotel was quite magnificent and wonderfully expensive. Given that they both came from one of the poorest quarters of Catania, it was comforting to think that they had arrived at a different and a better place, though she could at the same time sense his discomfort in being in a place where no one knew who he was, where he could so easily be mistaken for just another common working class Sicilian with money. They sat in the bar and sipped cocktails, which he didn't much like. He walked through the car park examining the cars and comparing them to his own (he had bought a new one, and now had a licence), a comparison he enjoyed. They looked out over the splendid gardens, and enjoyed the view of Mount Etna to their right and the mountains of Calabria across the sea to their left; and as it was May, there was still some gleaming traces of snow on the mountain top. They ate the food the hotel provided with great appreciation. In the mornings he swam fifty lengths of the pool; in the afternoon, they retired to their room, and he made love to her with single minded dedication, as he sensed he was expected to do.

This was the first time they had ever been entirely alone, and the experience was strange for both of them. She, to her surprise, missed her mother and father, and her sister; they had always been there, and now they were not; he too was away from the family that he had dominated since the death of his father. They were not here, there was only Stefania, a relative stranger, for they had only spent comparatively few hours in each other's company until now. It felt alien to be so close to someone, to be so entirely with one person. He felt taken aback when in the solitude of their bedroom she would stretch out her hand and touch his earlobe, or comment approvingly in the shape of his nose. These things had never mattered before. Coming out of the bathroom after a shower with his towel wrapped securely round his waist, he felt curiously naked and vulnerable.

They often talked about the child and thought about the child too. The birth would take place in less than three months, in July, at the very warmest time of the year. He felt sorry for her having to go into labour while Catania would be so hot, so airless. He was convinced they would have a son, who would be called Renato. She was happy with that name, his father's name, the Chemist's name, as long as he did not object to her being Isabella if a girl. But he could not quite reason himself into thinking it would be a girl. It had to be a boy; he could not imagine anything but a boy.

Sitting in the Roman Theatre of Taormina, walking that wonderful main street and admiring the views, seeing the Sicilian sky in abundance, the mountains and the sea, he was struck not by the beauty of it all, but by the contrast with his own place of birth, with Purgatory, the place where he and she had spent their entire lives. Here the rich came and paid twice the price for a cup of coffee that tasted exactly the same as the one you could buy in Catania; one day, he resolved, he would join the rich; indeed he was already well on his way there. She too wanted to be rich, to have the same taste as the rich, to have the same culture. Both in their own way felt the pain of exclusion and the desire to be admitted into the charmed circles that existed just beyond their reach.

They had brought books with them, and because there was so little to talk about, they both read in the evening, sitting on the hotel terrace. Rather to their surprise, they were the only two people who seemed to read in the entire hotel. He had brought with him the Confessions of Saint Augustine, which don Giorgio had given him as a perhaps ironic wedding present, and which he found utterly fascinating; he hadn't realised that the ancient Romans had been such interesting people. He was also reading a history of the Risorgimento, and found himself loathing Garibaldi and loathing his wife even more. The nineteenth century was clearly the century when everything had gone wrong, the century when Sicily had been incorporated into Italy, a place that did not care for it at all, and why? All to placate the vanity of one man and his bitch of a wife. Stefania had brought some books about art, one of which was a beautifully illustrated and compact book about Caravaggio, which he read too with great attention. He loved the colour reproductions of the paintings. He also loved the fact that Caravaggio had killed a man. He was secretly pleased to think that he owned quite a bit of art himself, including a Velasquez, the only pity being that it had to be hidden away in a cellar.

He wondered how the boys of the quarter were getting on in his absence. This was his first ever holiday, his first ever absence from Purgatory. Were they still stealing wallets and car radios, under the direction of Turiddu? Would they get into trouble without him there? Would he get back and find the place completely changed? Would the police have swept in, arrested everyone, and imposed law and order in place of the pleasing anarchy that generally ruled? God forbid that it should be so. He did not on the whole like this holiday: the enforced leisure, the lack of excitement, the constant company of his new wife – though this was hardly something he could explain to her. The sense of complete sexual satiation was also deeply alien. She was a passionate kisser and his lips were sore. His limbs ached, though that was not unpleasant. When the child was born, he hoped, she would have another focus for her attention, and she would be less fixed on him. And when they returned to Purgatory, he would have his work. He was not meant to be spoilt in this way. As the days passed, he began to look forward more and more to his return to Purgatory and his liberation from Taormina.

When they did get back, they went to their new house, the restructuring of which had kept Stefania very busy before the wedding, along with her dress and other matters. He deposited the suitcases in the living room, and looked out of the window into the square below, and admired the outline of the dome of the Church of the Holy Souls in Purgatory, and immediately felt the reassuring familiarity of home. There were the usual figures scattered around the square: one was Turiddu, smoking a cigarette. A moment later, Stefania came into the room, to find him gone and the door to the stairs open. She looked out of the window and saw her new husband in the square. Turiddu stood before him. Her husband pulled the cigarette out of the boy's astonished mouth, and trod it underfoot. Then, she saw, he made him empty his pockets, and reveal a packet of what were obviously cigarettes. Through the glass she heard raised voices. Calogero stamped on the cigarette packet, and slapped Turiddu in the face, hard. A small crowd had gathered, other boys looking on. Her husband's raised and infuriated voice continued. She knew he did not like smoking. Then he took Turiddu by the collar of his shirt, took off his own belt and began to thrash him mercilessly while the others watched. Welcome back to Purgatory, thought Stefania, as she looked on.

That July Calogero missed the birth of his daughter Isabella. She was born in the middle of the month, the very day on which Calogero was able to cement his rule over the quarter known as Purgatory. He hated smoking, as Turiddu had discovered, and he also hated other unhealthy things like drugs, and it turned out that one of the other men his own age, Ino, whom he had been at school with, had come into the quarter with the intention of selling drugs to the local boys. Several of the older boys, the ones who acted as his eyes and ears, in particular another man of his own age called Alfio, who had funny teeth, had told him this, and Turiddu had confirmed it by the simple expedient of buying some merchandise off Ino. Ino's supplier was from the other side of the city, but the arrival of a drug dealer, however young and inexperienced, was a threat not just to the wellbeing of the quarter, but to Calogero himself. In one of the narrow streets, late at night, he confronted Ino. A fight ensued, and knives were drawn. A crowd gathered to watch. Ino tried to stab Calogero in the buttock, the favoured target of the knifeman, not life-threatening, but certainly threatening to the opponent's prestige. Luckily Calogero was able to overcome him, and disarm him, suffering no more than a cut to the seat of his pants and a slight gaze of the flesh. He and Ino had been friends all their childhoods, but he could not tolerate a rival. If Ino thought mercy was to be shown him, he was wrong. Once he was on the ground, Calogero used his knife to cut away Ino's clothes, reducing him to his underpants. Then he and his helpers, which included Turiddu, thrashed Ino with their belts. The buckles of the belts bit into his flesh. Eventually the scourged man ran away.

It was not finished. Though at this point Rosario was sent to tell Calogero that his wife had been taken to hospital and that he should come at once, the younger brother was ignored. Calogero was too much intent on punishing Ino for his presumption, for his usurpation of his territory. With six or seven helpers, he went to the place where Ino lived with his parents, which, as it turned out, he owned. He informed them of their eviction. He refused to listen to their protests or their pleas. With the other boys to help him, he began to throw their belongings out of the fourth floor apartment into the street below. The fridge, flying through the night air, made a huge crash, as did the beds and the crockery. For days afterwards the narrow street was blocked with broken furniture and smashed plates. The rubbish remained as a reminder to all. Ino and his family were never seen again.

It was only several hours after Isabella was born that Calogero managed to visit his wife in hospital and see the new-born.

The violence against Ino did not represent a loss of temper or a surge of territorial pride, but rather a calculated repression of someone who had been a friend. The consequences were exactly as Calogero had hoped and expected. One of the men who habitually bought stolen car radios mentioned the matter a few days later. His message was discrete but unmistakeable. The person who had supplied Ino with the drugs that he had proposed to sell in Purgatory now realised that he had made a mistake and that Ino was a fool. Ino was now out of the picture. If anyone were to sell drugs to those who wanted to buy them in the Purgatory quarter, it should be Calogero or someone nominated by him. A weekly drop off in exchange for cash could be easily arranged. Calogero listened to this, heard what the sums involved would be – quite small, but profitable, and one had to start somewhere- and felt his previous hatred of the filth of drugs and the foulness of smoking drop away.

Chapter Four

Don Giorgio was not, for a priest, a particularly bad-tempered man; in fact he was much as most human beings are: the little things in life annoyed him the most; the big things, the major disappointments, and there had been many, he could handle with patience. He was philosophical about his failure to rise in the Church; he had a comfortable house, lots of books and the consolations of faith; he was the rector of a beautiful Church in which he could pray for the Holy Souls in Purgatory, an occupation that he found worthwhile and satisfying. (In his reading of Church History, nothing had shocked him more than the way Henry VIII had abolished monasteries and chantries on the grounds that praying for the dead was a waste of time, and the money set aside for that purpose better used by the King.) Really, his was the ideal job. And yet he knew he was a coward, and the case of Calogero proved it. He should have refused to preside at the Chemist's funeral; he should have refused to celebrate Calogero's wedding; and when Isabella was born, on the very night of the assault on Ino and his family, he should have refused to baptise her. He should have made Calogero an outcast, a pariah, in the eyes of the Church. He should have confronted the people of Purgatory and condemned them as the prophets of old would have done, and as some priests in certain parts of the island still did. (Though, he suspected, perhaps with some justification, that some of these social justice warriors were taking the positions they did in order to garner attention for themselves.) He, by contrast, had opted for the quiet life; but even in that quiet life there was a price to pay.

The case of Rosario continued to distress him. He was a very good boy in Don Giorgio's estimation. He was quiet and well behaved and devoted to the Church. His outward behaviour was excellent. He was good to his sisters and devoted to his mother. But Calogero did not value him, but subjected him to endless humiliation, that was clear. Calogero had taken the view that as their father was dead, he, Calogero, took the place of their father. Calogero also made it clear that he was a great believer in corporal punishment. He frequently took off his belt and thrashed whoever displeased him. Don Giorgio knew this. These beatings were public and hardly secret, as the case of Ino had proved. However, one day he had found Turiddu snivelling on the Church steps, and Turiddu had told him that he had displeased the boss, and the boss had punished him. But he had said this with almost a sense of pride.

Don Giorgio was stung by this and did something unusual. He took action. It seemed to him that Calogero's actions were not just wrong but also illegal. There were numerous things on the television about the protection of children, and numerous directives from the Church. It was a crime to mistreat a child and it was also a crime to do nothing when you had evidence that a child was being mistreated. Therefore, if only in his own interests, he ought to do something. He decided he would go and see Turiddu's father, which, as it turned out, was exactly the wrong thing to do.

He was admitted into the house warily; he was clearly not a welcome visitor, but coffee was made and he sat down with the father, while the mother, who knew what was coming by some instinct, left the room.

Turiddu's father gave the impression of being a small depressed old man, though he was in truth neither old nor small. He worked as a waiter in one of the restaurants on the Via Etnea. He seemed crushed by life.

'How is your son?' asked the priest.

'Father, he is thirteen and I can do nothing with him at all. He is beyond my control. He makes my life a misery. He is a thief and a liar. We have found things in his room which he cannot explain: wallets, credit cards, car radios, women's handbags. He must be stealing them and then he trades them with some man who comes to the quarter every week to take the stolen goods.'

'And who made your son into a thief?'

'Father, you know the answer.'

He nodded, he did.

'That man made him into a thief. But it gets worse; just recently we think Turi has been using drugs or selling drugs and Calogero di Rienzi is behind that too. And the worst thing of all: we think he has introduced him to one of the bad women of the quarter. You know what I mean. That man has taken my son's innocence away.'

Don Giorgio said: 'I think Calogero has been mistreating your son physically.'

'Yes,' he said. 'He hits him with a belt. That is what he does. We hear it. Caloriu comes here whenever he pleases. Sometimes he spends the entire night here in Turi's room. He says that he needs to get away from his wife and the baby who make a noise. We have heard him beating Turi. We heard that this morning.'

Don Giorgio suppressed the next question he was going to ask, namely, could they stop him? Could they ban him from the house? But he realised that they must have tried to stop him, and failed. Turiddu's father read his mind.

'This house is no longer my own. It belongs to Calogero. He threatened me in front of my son, and he carried out his threat. You have no children but you can imagine what that felt like. To be humiliated in front of my own son. He has ruined the boy's innocence; he has taken over my home; he has made me permanently afraid. He also did something else; he took the keys of the storeroom that belongs to this flat, in the basement. He uses that to store stolen goods, I am sure.'

'Can we not tell the police?' asked don Giorgio.

But even as he said this, he knew that it was hopeless. There was no need to discuss it. Who killed Vitale? They would never know, but it seemed clear that Calogero could easily have done so; and to tell the police would be to invite him to kill the informant or someone close to the informant. The family had suffered enough. There were other children whose future could not be risked. And the other question that hung between them – namely, could Turiddu somehow be detached from Calogero? – that too seemed hopeless. They were locked together in a dance of death. The only thing that could be done, it seemed to don Giorgio, was to stop other children falling into his clutches. But even there, it was too late. Every male child over the age of nine in the quarter followed him.

Don Giorgio left the apartment with a sense of sorrow and foreboding. What was to be done? He had assumed that when Calogero married his wife (whom he considered to be a vacuous creature) and left home for a home of his own, he would actually do that. But he was still spending time with Turiddu and he was soon not surprised to find out, through the simple expedient of asking, that Calogero had insisted that the second bed remain in the bedroom he shared with his younger brother, and that he slept there from time to time, claiming that the baby at home kept him awake at night, and that he needed a place of proper rest. Don Giorgio suspected that this was to keep an eye on his brother and to let him know that he would never leave him entirely alone. Sometimes Rosario would be yawning at the early Mass in the weekday and when asked would tell the priest that his brother had come into the bedroom and woken him up in the middle of the night.

The other thing that Don Giorgio now knew was the Calogero had forced his brother into lying. Thanks to what the lawyer Rossi had told him, he knew that the child – he had been twelve at the time – had lied to the police to establish his brother's alibi on the night of the fire at the hardware shop in Via Vittorio Emanuele. Moreover, the boy had had and still had a key to the street entrance of the church sacristy, so he could let himself into the church and set up for the early Mass. This fact and the existence of the storeroom full of stolen goods alerted him to the fate of the Spanish Madonna now sequestrated for the last three years.

One day he decided to question the boy.

'You keep the church key round your neck, don't you?' he asked.

'Yes, Father,' said Rosario.

'Did Calogero ever ask to borrow it?'

The boy went bright red. He could not lie. Calogero had not asked to borrow it. He never asked to borrow anything. He just took what he wanted.

'I was asleep. He took it off me when I was asleep,' he said.

'When did this happen?'

Once more, about this the boy could not lie. Calogero has taken the key off him at around the time the Spanish Madonna had disappeared. Don Giorgio did not blame Rosario for this, he blamed himself. He should have realised that something like this could happen, indeed would happen. Moreover, he knew that Rosario would never have surrendered the key willingly, and he remembered the child's grief when the theft of the painting had been discovered. Rosario had known at once what the police had never been able to work out.

Don Giorgio still mourned the loss of the Spanish Madonna, but now he knew almost for sure who the thief was; yet the matter was more complicated that it seemed, and not simply by the presence and involvement of Rosario. If Calogero had stolen it, it did not follow (despite the existence of the storeroom) that he still had it. He may well have sold it on, or destroyed it if it had proved impossible to sell on, and too hot to hold onto. But if they could get the picture back, this would, he was sure, do much to restore his standing, and the standing of the Confraternity, both of which had been dented by their failure to prevent the theft. The recovery of the picture would also do something to restore the bad reputation that the quarter enjoyed.

He knew he could only talk to one person, and he would have to be careful, lest he implicate Rosario in the theft. That person was the lawyer Petrocchi; the Confraternity had hundreds of members, who turned up in numbers only for the annual Mass of the Holy Souls on 2nd November. When it came to the business side of things, it was clear that only Petrocchi counted, or so everyone assumed.

He was an important man, and he could always ask to see him in his office. But that would not be right, sensed don Giorgio. Far better to wait for one of those rare occasions when Petrocchi came to the Church, and then use that as the opportunity for doing what he needed to do. There was no hurry. He had to act carefully and slowly. He had to make his approach seem natural. And so he waited for Petrocchi. The Spanish Madonna, he sensed, having been lost for almost four years, was, wherever she was, safe, if she had not come to harm already; her status as a kidnapped icon would not change.

In fact, he saw Petrocchi on the first day of November, the day before the feast of the Holy Souls. The head of the Confraternity came round to ask how preparations were going for the Mass the next day, and to remind the priest of the reception that would follow in one of the palaces on the Via Etnea, not that there was any need for that.

Petrocchi was in an expansive happy mood. Sensing his opportunity, don Giorgio listened to him enunciate the various things the Confraternity had done in the last year, not least of which was the finishing of the restoration of the Church's interior, which now looked magnificent. They stood before the high altar, and their eyes both rested on the ugly dark hole that marked the place where the Spanish Madonna had been. Petrocchi spoke of the ongoing project to commission either a photograph that would be indistinguishable from a painting, or a new painting, or a copy of the missing painting, to fill the hole. There were exponents of all three ideas in the Confraternity, and the matter, which had ground on for months, was yet to be resolved. He himself was in favour of a copy, though, at certain times, something new, something modern, seemed attractive.

'After all, there is no going back to the past,' he mused.

'But if we could go back to the past, wouldn't you want to?' asked don Giorgio.

Petrocchi sensed that something was in the offing, that something had been heard. He himself had made enquiries about getting the painting back. The Madonna had been sequestrated, kidnapped. No one wanted her more than they did. The ransom would be paid, but he had asked friends, and they had asked their friends, who in turn had asked their friends – the friends in Palermo – and no one knew anything. And if they did not know…. But he sensed the priest had something to tell him; slowly he let him bring the conversation round to the direction he wanted it to take. Petrocchi pretended that he did not realise this, though of course he did, and so did the priest. It was a little game they played, a pretence they maintained, so that what came out, which was carefully prepared, might seem natural and by the way.

By this time they were in the priest's house, in his study, sharing a bottle of grappa.

'The truth is,' confided don Giorgio, 'that people have been talking, and after the event, long after the event, people admit what they assume, and that assumption is taken for certainty. The Spanish Madonna…. How her absence breaks my heart! She was stolen by that man Calogero di Rienzi. He did it to insult me, he was a boy at the time, well, I am a priest, I am used to insults. But he did it to insult the Confraternity, to show that he is not afraid of all the important people who are members, the princes, the dukes, the university professors, the lawyers, and of course, you.'

'What makes you so sure it was him?' asked the lawyer Petrocchi.

'The way the man acts. He is laughing at us all.'

Petrocchi conceded this point with a nod.

'That is bad,' he said. 'Very bad. I don't know the man, but I have heard of him, naturally enough. A man who works in my firm, Rossi, he deals with his affairs. But where is the Madonna?'

'Where are all the objects stolen from churches?' asked the priest. 'There have been so many thefts. It is surprising they haven't stolen the relics of Saint Agatha herself.'

'They are very securely guarded.'

'And we cannot guard everything,' said don Giorgio. 'Somewhere this man keeps a hoard of stolen goods, I think. He owns a lot of properties. They should all be searched.'

'His property business is legal,' said the lawyer. 'So far as I have heard, the rest of his business is all small fry. He thinks he's important, but is he? Perhaps he should be taught a lesson. So he does not laugh at his betters.'

'You are forgetting the case of Vitale, the man who died in the fire at the hardware shop in Via Vittorio Emanuele,' said the priest. 'And do not forget who his father was.'

'That is a lot of talk. There's very little evidence, only rumour.'

'But,' said the priest, before they were distracted by that, 'It is not Calogero but his brother I want to talk to you about. You remember the procession on Holy Souls day last November? He was the one who organised it all really. He has been serving Mass here since he was eight years old, very devotedly. He is now in his early teens. He's works hard at school. Most of the boys from round here of his age don't go to school any more. He's clever. He is a very good boy, I assure you, not like his brother at all. Not like his father either! Anyway, this young man, Rosario, wants to become a priest. He has thought about it, prayed about it, and that is what he wants. God is calling him.'

'What exactly is it you want to do, don Giorgio?' asked the lawyer, cutting him off.

'I want you to help me to get him away from this place, and in particular from his brother Calogero. I want him to go to a junior seminary in somewhere like Bergamo – far away. Still in Italy, but in a different world. I have got several places in mind.'

'And where do I come into this?' asked the lawyer.

'In two ways. Firstly, the family have no income apart from the 500 euro a month they get from the Confraternity. Calogero is rich, but he does not help them, as far as I can see, or chooses not to. He would never pay. When the father died, Calogero got all the money, all the properties, quite how I do not know.'

Petrocchi ignored this, which meant, don Giorgio thought, that he did know.

'And the other way?'

'He would need a letter of recommendation from the priest who knows him well, which is no problem, but also from the Vocations Director of the

Archdiocese of Catania, if he were to enter a minor seminary. I have not sent Rosario to him, and have not put him through the usual process. I fear they will refuse to co-operate. They are very touchy about anyone who might have even a whiff of criminality about them. You may remember the way I was hauled in over the funeral of the Chemist. As Rosario is the son of the Chemist and the brother of Calogero di Rienzi, they may well feel they do not want him as a future priest of the diocese of Catania. They may treat the boy as if he were the criminal, not his brother. They exaggerate, of course. The real criminals pass freely in our midst, are feted and admired by everyone. They walk down the Via Etnea and everyone says hello to them. But this poor boy is likely to fall victim to their enthusiasm to show their whiter than white credentials.'

The lawyer considered. He felt suddenly weary. 'I can see their point. They don't want a criminal getting his family connection anywhere near the Church. A bit late in the day to try that tack, if you don't mind me saying. It is far too late. But there is always this desire to try and repair the damage long after the damage is done. But maybe you are looking in the wrong place. It might be best for the boy himself that he goes someone new, completely away from here, to America even, where he will not be known as the son of the Chemist. A fresh start. I can understand you wanting to get him away from his brother. There are boarding schools. Some expensive, some less so, that might suit him. Why shouldn't the Confraternity pay? I could persuade them. It would be seen as a favour to you and you have never asked for a favour before now. The English have good boarding schools. They have boarding schools that teach in English on the island of Malta. But first I think I should meet the young man. I mean I have seen him. But I should like to assess him myself, so that I can then make a recommendation to the Confraternity based on some personal knowledge.'

Don Giorgio knew that the Confraternity would do whatever the lawyer Petrocchi told them to do; but he admired this humble pretence that Petrocchi was merely the Confraternity's servant, and that he could only recommend, not command.

'That would be very kind. And yet I feel that there are no fresh starts in life. We live with our past wherever we go. Rosario will always be the son of the Chemist. It is how he handles that that matters. He is handling it excellently so far. Didn't the son of Martin Bormann become a priest? Did they make him hide? We all have to confront our pasts, where we come from, what we have done. One can go to America, but people from here who do that take Sicily with them. But the idea of a boarding school is a good one.'

And so it was that Rosario was eventually summoned to see the lawyer Petrocchi. Don Giorgio warned him what to expect, and reminded him to wear the suit he had worn for his confirmation in the Cathedral the previous year, and which luckily still fitted him. Their meeting took place in early summer, just after Rosario had finished his exams at school. He would be fifteen that summer.

Petrocchi always had lunch in an ordinary restaurant not far from his office which stood on the Via Etnea, and Rosario was asked to present himself there at 1.30pm at the lawyer's table. He had seen Petrocchi many times at functions in the Church of the Holy Souls in Purgatory, but never spoken to so exalted a figure; he recognised his short dumpy frame, his greying hair. Petrocchi managed a smile of welcome when he approached and motioned for him to sit.

'I always eat the same things. It saves me having to choose. Will the same do for you?' he said.

'Certainly, sir.'

Petrocchi glanced at the waiter, who immediately understood.

'How do you like life in Purgatory?' asked the lawyer.

'I have never lived anywhere else, sir, so how can I know any different? I cannot really make a judgement.'

'It's interesting,' said Petrocchi when the lasagne came. 'There is a statistics office in Rome, which produces facts and figures for every commune in the country: so if you want to know which is the richest place, well, it is somewhere in Lombardy, I think; or which is the least healthy place, it is somewhere in Campania, I think. Or which is the most educated place, the place with the highest concentration of degree holders, and so on. And the picture that emerges does not surprise you at all. In fact, it reinforces your prejudices, which, to my mind is bad; statistics should challenge you. The further north you go the better it gets, and the further south you go, the opposite- that is the picture. The most crime ridden place is Scampia in Naples; the place with the most murders is just outside Palermo. But the worst place for big crime, white collar crime, is Milan; though most people would say that the worst city for crime is Rome, the seat of government, and that government is just an extortion racket.'

'Saint Augustine said that government without morality is a latrocinium, a conspiracy of thieves.'

'And that was how long ago?'

'He died in 430 AD, sir.'

'And nothing has changed. That is the key thing to understanding our nature. Nothing changes, people do not change, people cannot change, Sicily will never change.'

'The Leopard,' said Rosario.

'Quite right. You are well read for one so young. That is good. The Leopard is not an easy book to read. The film was marvellous. Anyway, to go to statistics, they are published for region, province, commune, but never for small districts in a commune. Now, if you were to look at Purgatory nationally, it would win, I would not be surprised, in all categories: the most ignorant people, the greatest number of children who do not go to school, the worst petty crime, the worst public services – roads and street lighting, things like that. But as it is so small, no one has done a study of it. But I can prove to you that it is the worst place in Catania and possibly all Sicily, because the rents per square metre are the lowest. I think that is something that proves the point. Many of the buildings are abandoned. This means, building on your father's work, your brother- how old is he now?'

'Nineteen.'

'Will be a millionaire many times over by the time he is thirty.' Petrocchi said this with a sense of resignation which concealed a hint of jealousy. 'And it will all be completely legal, more or less. You see, he is buying up derelict properties, properties that no one wants, properties that people find hard to sell. Soon he will own the whole quarter. He uses the lawyer Rossi for this sort of work. Now some of the previous owners have been more or less persuaded to sell against their better judgement. But he persuaded them. Others could not wait to take the money and run, because they feared that their properties were losing value by the day, which they were. After all, if your dark and narrow street becomes a haven for robbers, then no one wants to live there, and the dark and narrow street is an object of fear, not thought of as picturesque at all. And there is one whole street that is full of prostitutes of the very lowest kind – no one would want to live there. He buys properties and then he rents them out to the lowest of the low, and the whole place becomes more and more of a slum. But then, in a few years' time, he will turf them all out, do the places up, and hey presto you have an elegant and fashionable new quarter a few metres from the Via Etnea, in easy reach of the station too.'

'Isn't it hard to evict people who have lived there for a long time?'

'Yes, Rosario. Legal evictions are long and tedious affairs. The other type, not so much. For them he will use the nasty little teenage criminals he cultivates.'

'But then.....'

'Precisely. I see that you can work it out. When he gets rid of the prostitutes, and the pickpockets and the thieves, he will have no further use for his criminal friends. Then he will get rid of them. That might not be so easy. People like them will be hard to shake off. They might want their rewards. They might not be the sort of people who you want to associate with when you are so very rich. This boy who is your age...'

'Turiddu?'

Rosario was shocked that the lawyer Petrocchi had heard of him.

'Yes....' Petrocchi could see that Rosario was surprised. 'That nasty little baggage has been arrested several times. And every time he gets arrested, your brother sends a lawyer to get him out of trouble. Not the lawyer Rossi, no one who works for my firm. A criminal lawyer, the sort who is used to representing lowlifes. But word gets about. No one is allowed to touch Calogero's protégé. Which makes you think – why does Calogero value him so much? A kid your age? A wallet thief? Surely someone who if sent off to the reformatory at Bicocca could be replaced several times over? A nasty child. Perhaps that is the reason. The last time he was rescued from the police it was for causing actual bodily harm with a knife.'

'He stabbed someone?'

'In the course of a robbery. Not very seriously. But still.'

'But why did the police not charge him?'

'You would think that our police forces would want someone like him off the streets. But they may think that someone like Turiddu would soon be replaced. And he soon would. And then, they are amenable to persuasion. The lawyer turns up, mentions he has been retained by Calogero di Rienzi, and they know that if they let the child off with a caution, Calogero will be grateful. Likewise, the offended party is told that if they do not press charges, they will be on the receiving end of Calogero's gratitude. So, the boy is in the police station, and on the promise of a few hundred euros, he is let go. Works every time.'

'That is why we are in the mess we are. Because no one can trust the police,' said Rosario.

'Quite,' said the lawyer. 'Perhaps you should become a lawyer. It is an uphill struggle being honest at the best of times, but when you are surrounded by criminals.....' The waiter came and took away their plates. Soon two veal cutlets appeared, along with a side dish of spinach. 'But the truth of the matter is that one day Calogero will look at his little friend Turiddu and think he has no further need for him, and get rid of him.'

'Oh, he can't do that,' said Rosario without thinking.

'You mean Turiddu knows too much, and that he would be a threat? All the more reason for him to end up with a broken neck down one of the craters of Mount Etna. Or bobbing in the sea, off Giardini Naxos. Sometimes useful people need to be disposed of because their uses have come to an end, and they cannot be safely retired. One should always beware of making oneself indispensable. My dear child, don't you realise that that was what happened to your father?'

Rosario looked at the lawyer blankly.

'You mean they killed him?' he asked at last.

'It is one of the theories. Because in this place no one, absolutely no one, ever believes anything just happens by accident. Of course, he could have blown himself up by accident. But it is also possible that having worked for them for so long, having done so many jobs for them, they decided it would be best to cover their traces.'

'And my brother will do the same with Turiddu?'

'Of that I am certain. And it is important that you know why this is important for you. When your brother has made his fortune and becomes a respectable man – and please remember that all fortunes started in ways that were a little murky – when Calogero changes, he will need not people like Turiddu, but people like you.'

'Sir, he will never change. He can't change. His methods are never legal but always violent. He acts by force, not force of law. And he will never get rid of Turi or someone like him; there are plenty of them; they are joined at the hip. And he would not want to. He takes pleasure in violence. He likes being feared.'

'So, you are not tempted?'

'Even if I could be, no, I am not tempted. Some people enjoy violence. I do not.'

'You do not want to be rich?' asked the lawyer. 'Most people do.'

The boy shook his head. 'It didn't help my father, did it?' Then he asked: 'Did they really kill him?'

'Their motives are always hard to discern,' said the lawyer Petrocchi. 'But in this case, I think it is probable, even certain, that his death was an accident. If they had wanted to kill him, they would have done so in a quieter way. His death made headlines. That wasn't good for them. The police are still investigating. They do not like that.'

'What are they investigating?'

'As they must have told you shortly after it happened, they have been drawing up a list of all the mysterious explosions in Italy in the last twenty years, and trying to link that up with your father's movements over the last twenty years. In theory this should produce a pattern of assassinations. They then hope to see whose interest was served and work out who ordered these assassinations. It might have been one person, it might have been several. It was quite possible that your father worked for whoever paid him; he could have worked for them some of the time, and for other people the rest of the time, people such as the secret services, other branches of government. But the truth is it has been impossible to reconstruct your father's movements. He naturally told no one where he was going. He kept nothing written down; he travelled by train, and paid for his tickets in cash. He may have had a car in Italy, but no one has found it. Well, they may have found it and removed it, not realising its significance. He stayed in places, but it seems they gave him several false identities to use when checking into hotels, though on the day he died he had checked in using his real identity. Or he may simply have slept in his car, if he had one. Frankly, I have heard from people close to the investigation, that they have been working on this for three years and making no progress at all. It is one tiny thread in a much larger investigation.'

'I remember the policemen who interviewed me. They were called Storace and Volta.'

'Storace has retired, I think, and gone back to where he came from; he wasn't from Sicily. Volta is still involved in the investigation. They say he is a clever man. He must realise how futile the whole thing is. Every year the investigation grows; every year it makes less and less progress, swallows more and more man hours and resources. In the end, everyone throws their hands up in the air and despairs. That is how it will end. But tell me – how do you feel, being the Chemist's son?'

'Luckily, I never knew until he died that I was the Chemist's son; I never knew while he was alive that my father was a mass murderer. But now I know, I reject and renounce him utterly. I was never particularly fond of him, as he was never at home. Now he is dead, I am happy. He died as he lived. He was killed in the way he killed so many. I am horrified by his coldness, and I see the same coldness in Caloriu. He does not care about what happens to others. As for my mother, sir, she shut her eyes to my father and she still shuts her eyes.'

'She shuts her eyes to the truth about Calogero?'

'Of course she does. But she knows. As she must have known with my father. My father at least pretended to be an itinerant whatever it was. Caloriu makes no attempt to hide his depravity. He advertises it. That is what makes him powerful. He will stop at nothing. He has stopped at nothing. He killed Vitale.'

Petrocchi nodded. He had found out what he wanted to find out. The main course was over.

'Well', he said, 'If you want to go abroad to study at a boarding school, the Confraternity will pay. Educating you would not be a waste of money. How about going to the school run by the Christian Brothers in Rome? It is right next to the Spanish Steps. Alternatively, you could go to England or to Malta. Even America. I will look out for the details, forward them to don Giorgio, and he will help you choose. But the choice is yours.'

'It will be a wonderful opportunity, sir. Thank you very much.'

'And each summer, when you come home from school, you will work as an intern in my office,' concluded the lawyer. 'That is part of the bargain.'

'Yes, sir.'

He gestured for coffee.

After lunch, Rosario, who had taken the day off school, went for a walk towards the Cathedral. He lingered in the square outside, admiring the elephant and the fountain, and then went in to admire the chapel of the relics of Saint Agatha. Now that it seemed likely that he would be leaving the city of his birth, the only city he had ever known, Catania had never seemed so enchanting or so beautiful. But as he left the Cathedral, he found that he had a text message from his mother asking him to return home as soon as he could. With a sigh, he retraced his steps towards Purgatory.

His mother but rarely used her mobile phone to summon him, and he took the steps up to the flat they lived in two at a time. He opened the door, and walked in but sensed his mother's absence almost immediately. She was always home, and her presence was tangible, perhaps because of the associated smell of cooking, or the ambient sounds that surrounded her. But she was clearly out, he felt, as he stepped into the kitchen, and so too were his two sisters. The house, always such a female space, was empty. Except it wasn't. There in the kitchen, leaning against the wall, was his brother. And on the other side of the room was Turiddu. Between them was the complicit silence of complete understanding.

Rosario felt his stomach constricted, an unpleasant reminder of the very pleasant lunch he had had only two hours ago. He looked at his brother, as if to ask for an explanation of Turiddu's presence, and his mother's absence.

'I sent her and the girls away. They will be back tonight,' said Calogero quietly. 'You look ridiculous in that suit. I don't think you will want to wear it again after this. In fact, you will want to throw it away, because it will just bring you bad memories. You have disobeyed me.'

'How?' asked Rosario, conscious that Turiddu was now behind him, and had shut the kitchen door and placed a chair in front of it, on which he sat.

'You went and met the lawyer Petrocchi without telling me, and you discussed family things with him. There's no point denying it. The waiter heard you, and he told another waiter there who is one of our boys. You were talking to Petrocchi about our father, whose most unworthy son you are. Didn't I warn you never to talk about family things? That time you spoke to the police?'

Rosario was dumb. How much had been overheard? The best thing to do was to say nothing. Any admission might be something more than Calogero assumed. He remembered now that he had told Petrocchi that Calogero had killed Vitale. If Calogero knew this or guessed it… he felt Calogero might kill him. The best thing was silence. Besides, any pleading would be ignored and would only add to the humiliation. He sensed now what the humiliation was to be: Calogero was going to beat him in front of Turiddu.

Calogero looked at Turiddu, who was behind Rosario; Turiddu understood and came up to the boss, and removed his belt – a thick leather strap, equipped with a heavy metal buckle – and put it in the hands of Calogero.

He then went back to his seat, to watch. With an almost imperceptible smile, Calogero advanced and took hold of his brother and pressed him face downwards against the kitchen table, holding him by the neck with his left hand. With his right hand he pulled down his brother's trousers, exposing his bare flesh. Turiddu sniggered. Rosario knew not to struggle or cry out, but nothing prepared him, even though he had suffered it many times before, for the searing pain and noise of Calogero's belt hitting him on the back of the legs and the buttocks. The belt's heavy brass buckle bit into his flesh. He tried desperately not to make any noise, knowing that any sound of distress would only feed Calogero's appetite for inflicting pain.

At length the beating stopped. Calogero was breathless, and Rosario could see, as he righted himself, sweating. Turiddu, meanwhile, was smiling. He had had quite a few beatings from the boss in his time, but never anything like that. Calogero lightly threw the belt back to him. He put it on, wiping away the traces of blood on the buckle against the side of his jeans. Neither of them said anything.

Rosario, miserably pulling up his trousers, realised that it was not over.

'You were also speaking about Turiddu,' said Calogero at length.

Rosario was now unable quite to remember what had been said about Turiddu, but knew it was nothing complementary.

Turiddu stood up slowly from his sitting position and looked at him. Both boys were the same age, though Turiddu was the smaller. But whereas Turiddu had been in lots of fights, and won them, Rosario had been in none at all. Calogero turned to the kitchen sink and put the plug in and turned on the taps. The water ran for a little while. Then Calogero stood back, and took the chair.

Rosario wondered what was happening, but only for a moment. Turiddu flew at him, and pulled him over to the sink, forcing his head under the water. He struggled in vain. Just when he thought he would lose consciousness, Turiddu released him, and allowed him to take a great gasping painful breath, just for a moment, before submerging him again. Again and again his head was rammed down into the sink and held under water, while half a breath was allowed him just before he thought he would expire.

How long this went on for, he was not sure. But eventually, it stopped. He was allowed to collapse onto the kitchen floor, barely conscious, choking. But it was not over yet. Turiddu, with a torrent of insults, fell upon him, and, with his mother's kitchen scissors, began to cut off his soaking clothes. Very soon he was naked and helpless on the floor. The remains of his suit, his shoes, his shirt, his underwear, were bunched up in a corner of the room; still the water flowed into the sink and over it, a horrible accompaniment to his torture, one that he would always from now on associate with this moment.

The tap was switched off. That was Calogero's work, who now looked down on him with dispassionate interest.

'Go on,' he said to Turiddu.

Permission given, Turiddu stood above his victim, and said: 'I need to take a piss.'

Rosario felt the hot liquid pour over him. Worse was to follow.

'Now I need to take a shit,' said Turiddu, 'and I know the perfect place.'

He held Rosario's nose, forcing him to open his mouth. Rosario sensed what was coming and tried to struggle, but Calogero held him down, which Turiddu lowered his trousers and defecated into his mouth, and then applied pressure to make him swallow it.

Then they left him alone while he choked and went to the sink, was sick, and tied his best to wash the filth out of his mouth. Behind him, Turiddu was going through the draw where the knives were kept, selecting a suitable instrument.

'I am going to cut off your miserable balls,' he said. 'Then I will let you go to the hospital on your own, just as you are. And we will see if you make it that far, or if they can save you.'

Calogero laughed as Rosario, covered in water, vomit, urine and faeces, tried to squirm away along the floor while Turiddu seized him by the ankles. He took an ankle while Turiddu held the other with his left hand and the knife with his right.

'How do I do it?' said Turiddu.

'Easy. You split the scrotum with the knife, then you lift out each ball and cut it off. Go on.'

Rosario began to howl.

'Wait,' said Calogero. 'I want to ask him something. I had better do it now. Did you tell Petrocchi that I killed Vitale?'

'Yes,' screamed Rosario.

There was silence.

'Good,' said Calogero. He put out a gentle hand to stay the knife.

A moment later, Rosario realised that he was alone.

Chapter Five

That Rosario di Rienzi had left home and taken refuge in the house of don Giorgio rapidly became the talk of the quarter, given that he was the younger brother of Purgatory's most famous son, Calogero di Rienzi. To leave home, to run away, at scarcely the age of fifteen, was an act of supreme rebellion, and disobedience, and to be condemned as such. But at the same time, one wondered what exactly was the cause of his flight; and one assumed that the cause was interesting to say the least, because no one was talking about it, not Rosario, not his brother, and not the priest or the mother of the two brothers.

Two days after his sudden defection, his mother came to see him, to plead with him to come home. Don Giorgio admitted her, and she and Rosario sat in the priest's small parlour while the lady made her case. She wept, she pleaded, she begged Rosario to come home, but he was stony faced, and refused to be moved. There was so much he could say, but he chose, carefully, not to say it. He chose not to say it because he knew that whatever he said, she would either deny it, or refuse to understand it.

For years she had known that Calogero beat him, and she had done nothing about it, except perhaps turn up the sound of the television to prevent herself hearing what was happening behind the bedroom door. Moreover, she had co-operated with this latest beating, summoning him home by text message (unless Calogero had done that, but even so, she must have realised that it was her phone he had used) and then vacating the house so that Calogero could have his opportunity. And it was worse: she had not asked a single question about what had really happened; she had not asked because she did not want to know; but she had seen the scene in the kitchen, the water, the other things, the torn and soaking clothes. What did she assume had happened? But she would not ask. The reality was too much for her. Instead she begged him to come home, because if he didn't the neighbours would speak about it, and people would look at her and her daughters and think badly of her.

He cut her off with a question:

'Did Caloriu send you? Does Caloriu want me to come back?'

'I want you to come back.'

'To protect you from Caloriu?'

She shook her head and wept. She knew about her eldest son, that was clear, and her tears were an admission in Rosario's eyes that she had sacrificed the interest of her other children to the interests of the eldest son. He felt almost sorry for her. There was no turning back for her; her life had become fixed ever since she had missed the opportunity of leaving her husband, if that opportunity had ever existed. Perhaps it had, for a fleeting moment, if ever the suspicion had ever entered her darkened mind that he was an evil man; but she had put that suspicion to rest, and in that decision she had fixed her destiny and assured the loss of her younger son. He felt almost sorry for her, but there was a hardness in his judgement, just as there perhaps had been in hers; she had chosen the easy way, the way too of less sympathy for the suffering, and she had given Calogero's victims no thought, her husband's victims no thought either. They had been shut out of her mind. She had shut him out, and now it was easier to shut her out. There was nothing now between them. At the age of fifteen he had lost his mother. But he had never really had her in the first place.

His sisters too, he knew, were now lost to him, which was sad, as he was fond of them, but they would do as their mother said, and as Calogero said. For the truth was that in leaving home he was doing a terrible thing. He was turning his back on everything he had known (his mother, who had used this phrase, was completely correct.) But to carry on living like this was more than he could bear to contemplate. The first day he had walked to school from the priest's house, he had seen Turiddu watching from the other side of the square, and make an obscene gesture in his direction. That he could live with. What could Turiddu do to him now, having done what he had already done? He had exhausted his armoury of assault. He was no longer frightened of him; rather he was frightened of what he himself might become if he surrendered to these people. To be like Turiddu was the greatest horror imaginable. And he remembered what the lawyer Petrocchi had said: that one day Calogero would find Turiddu surplus to requirements and throw him down Mount Etna, or drown him off Giardini Naxos.

In fact he felt more sorry for Turiddu, a person he hardly knew, than for his own mother. His mother, in her heart of hearts, knew what she had chosen; she had deliberately chosen not to sympathise with him. But Turiddu had little idea, he feared, about what awaited him. He was intoxicated by the success of his criminal career for the moment. But what would follow? How would he feel as his head was held under water in the sea? How would he feel as he his neck was broken and his body thrown into the crater? In those final moments would he regret the path he had chosen? Or was he incapable of regret? Was the thrill of the now more involving than any thought of the future? Would his death be a single moment in an otherwise wonderful life, which would not invalidate that life at all?

He wondered if Calogero would come and see him. He told don Giorgio (who had received a curtailed account of his assault) that Calogero should not be denied the house, and that he was not frightened to see him. In fact, he rather thought that Calogero was frightened of him, not the other way around. His flight, his declaration of independence, was something that Calogero could hardly have foreseen. After all, the whole Calogero project was predicated on the indissolubility of family ties, as well as the supposition that in the end no one could do without Calogero. He was a necessary thing, a necessary evil. He had made himself such. For Calogero to come round and threaten him, or to plead with him even, would be to undermine this basic claim, that people, especially his own family, needed Calogero more than he needed them. Calogero would bet on him coming back of his own accord, admitting his folly.

But he had no intention of doing this. Luckily, the project of his going to study abroad was still going ahead. Abroad, for him, started beyond the straits of Messina. He would soon be on the other side of the narrow seas, and when one crossed the straits, one landed in another world. In consultation with don Giorgio and with Petrocchi, he was going to go to school in Rome, and board with a family who took in foreign students, and who were known to don Giorgio, and he was going to go as soon as possible. Naturally, where he was going was kept a secret. And one day, suddenly, he was gone.

The fact was reported to Calogero, that one morning Rosario had been seen leaving with a suitcase and getting into a taxi, which, one assumed, took him to the airport. It had surprised him. He took it as a setback. People would now look at him as the man who had driven his own brother away. But the reaction of two people struck him. The first was Turiddu, who could not hide his satisfaction at the flight of Rosario. His puny little chest almost seemed to expand at the thought of it, though nothing was said – but one could know what he was thinking. That in itself was slightly annoying. One did not want the boy to get inflated ideas of his own importance. What Turiddu was too stupid to realise was that the sight of him torturing Rosario was perhaps not the best memory picture one could have of him. It made one realise what a monster Turiddu was.

His mother said nothing about Rosario, but his wife did. That surprised him.

'It seems to me,' said Stefania, 'that if Rosario and Turiddu quarrelled' (this was something that the whole quarter assumed) 'then you came down on the wrong side.'

He looked at her in surprise.

'What the hell do you know about it?' he asked.

'Rather more than you think, my dear,' she said, without looking up from the magazine she was reading.

He did not ask for elucidation, but he looked at her with new eyes. Perhaps she was not as stupid as he thought she was.

To change the subject, he approached where she sat, and took her hand. She looked up from her magazine.

'What?' she asked.

Her brazen smile, her crip question, withered him. He withdrew his hand.

'Nothing,' he said.

She smiled once more. He looked away. In a few moments the child Isabella would be waking up. They had not made love since her birth, now over two years ago.

A few months passed, summer retreated, and one afternoon, when the cooler weather came, while taking some air in the Villa Bellini after lunch, the lawyer Petrocchi met Calogero di Rienzi. Petrocchi was sitting on a bench in the sunshine, before going back to his office on the Via Etnea, when he saw, at the bottom of one of the alleys, a familiar figure coming towards him. He knew Calogero, he had seen him in the distance, but they had never spoken. He steeled himself to keep his cool, while noting that the gardens were rather empty; but he reassured himself that if Calogero wanted to kill him, he would have done so by now. Rosario had been gone for some time.

Calogero came and sat down at the end of the same bench.

'Hello,' he said. 'We have not met, but you know who I am and I know who you are.'

Their eyes did not meet, but Petrocchi inclined his head.

'I have never thanked you for the Confraternity's kindness in giving my mother a pension of 500 euros a month after my father died. It was very discretely done.'

Again, Petrocchi bowed his head in acknowledgement.

'Where did the authorisation of that payment come from?' asked Calogero mildly.

'You know where it came from,' said Petrocchi.

'Then why am I asking?'

'Because you want to hear me admit that I know. There is only one possible source. You know that. I know that. Who else could it be? I have nothing to do with the accounts of the Confraternity. That is left to accountants. They could perhaps give you a name, but that name will mean very little. But we all know where the power is. It is in Palermo.'

'It is in Palermo,' echoed Calogero. 'And there are numerous barriers, shall we say, between you and it; numerous shells, numerous false identities. To protect them; and to protect you.'

'I have never met them, I do not want to meet them, and I hope I never shall,' said Petrocchi. 'Ah,' he said, as if something had only just occurred to him. 'This is not because of your brother. You do not want to speak about that, do you? About how we got him away from you?'

'We could speak about that in due course,' said Calogero.

'But right now, it is the friends of the friends of the friends in Palermo that interest you, isn't it?' said Petrocchi. 'You are just a small-time crook, and you want to meet the people who control the big game, don't you?'

Calogero laughed.

'I know all about you,' said the lawyer with unaccustomed venom.

'Are you so sure?' asked Calogero mildly. 'Are you going to tell me it is all illegal? It is a man who works in your office, Rossi, who ensures that it is not.'

Petrocchi overcame his sudden surge of disgust for the man. For better or for worse, he had to live with such types. It was already compromising that he was Rossi's client. In addition, he knew Calogero could make trouble for the Confraternity, for the Church of the Holy Souls in Purgatory, and for don Giorgio. He remembered what had happened to Vitale. He made a conscious effort to be polite to this piece of shit, this dangerous man in their midst. This was what one had to put up with in society, the criminals hiding in plain view. One had to make compromises; one was already compromised. After all, here he was speaking to a murderer in the park; here he was, head of a Confraternity that paid out pensions on behalf of the friends in Palermo. And here he was, suddenly thinking of what personal advantage he could bring to himself, if he were to use his contact with this thug well. He was, he realised, already deep in; and the current temptation was too good to resist.

'Where is the Spanish Madonna?' asked Petrocchi.

'Why do you think I would know?'

'You know, because you stole it. Come, come, be honest. I know you stole it. Don Giorgio guessed you stole it.'

'Because my brother told him?'

'You had access to the key to the Church. And there was no sign of a break in.'

'There were thirty people with keys. Come now, you are a lawyer. You would never expect me to admit to doing such a thing, would you?'

Against his wishes, Petrocchi smiled.

'I want the picture back,' he said. 'And I know what you want. You want an introduction. As a lawyer, you would never expect me to admit that I knew the people you want to know, or even knew their intermediaries.'

Calogero laughed.

'Let no one admit anything,' he said. 'If I get what I want, then you will get what you want. I promise you. But there is something else too.'

'Ah,' said Petrocchi. There was always something else. 'You want to know where your brother has gone? I won't tell you.'

'I could easily find out, if I cared. But I do not want to know where Rosario has gone. Why should I? No, I want something that really is easy to give. I want to be a member of the Confraternity.'

'Is that all?' said Petrocchi, oblivious to the terrible mistake he was making. 'Why not? Consider it done. At least if you are a member of the Confraternity, we can rest assured that the Church is not going to be burned down, the collection is not going to be stolen, and none of us are going to be assaulted.' He paused. 'The day the Spanish Madonna returns to her home, then you can join the Confraternity.'

'Then it is all arranged,' said Calogero. 'I get the introduction. You get the picture. I get inducted into the Most Noble and Ancient Confraternity of the Holy Souls in Purgatory.'

He stood up.

'We shall be seeing a great deal of each other in years to come,' he remarked, before slowly moving away.

As soon as he left, Petrocchi was left with the feeling that perhaps he had not got the best part of the bargain. Introducing this man to the Confraternity would take a bit of brass neck on his part. After all the Most Noble and Ancient Confraternity had a certain social cachet. All the local nobility and most of the lawyers were members; but there were also lesser people, and it was a Catholic organisation, open to all. But a controller of pickpockets and a brothel keeper? But Calogero would not be those forever. And he comforted himself with the thought that if the Spanish Madonna returned to her rightful place under his watch, then he could more or less put Satan himself up for membership, and no one would mind. His prestige would be immense. There had been lots of publicity surrounding the theft. There would be huge publicity surrounding the recovery, and he himself would make sure he was right in the middle of it.

Far harder was complying with Calogero's request of the introduction. He himself did not know the friends in Palermo. He had taken care not to. He did not even acknowledge their existence. Of course people he knew, knew people, who knew people, who knew the friends. But to make enquiries now would be awkward and it might entail calling in a few favours. But then there was the picture. That was of incomparable value; making a few enquiries would cost him nothing. There would be a sense of justice in the kidnapped painting returning home. Coupled with the recent restoration of the Church, which had cost millions – all would redound to the glory of Petrocchi. And a little bit of glory would certainly be a useful insurance policy against future disaster.

Before Petrocchi's time, the Confraternity had been infiltrated by the friends from Palermo; this had been done by the one set of people who were the real power in the Confraternity, though not its members – its accountants. One always had to follow the money, he knew.

The Confraternity owned several properties in Catania and elsewhere which were supposed to provide for the upkeep of the Church of the Holy Souls in Purgatory and its priest. Many of these properties were now very valuable and their rents had spiralled. For example, the bar in which Petrocchi habitually had coffee near his office now paid some 20,000 euro a month rent to the Confraternity. At least on paper. The friends from Palermo pumped in about 12,000 a month into the bar, which was then channelled to the Confraternity and laundered in the process. The Confraternity's rents went towards certain legitimate things such as paying not very much to don Giorgio, as well as the until recently much neglected maintenance of the building's fabric; the rest, which was considerable, rested in the bank and in investments, and disbursements were made to 'widows and orphans', a charity which was foreseen by the Confraternity's constitution. Except of course that these widows and orphans had nothing or very little to do with the Confraternity itself. Most of them seemed to live outside Catania. And whose widows were they, whose orphans? Petrocchi knew the truth without having to dig for it. The Confraternity had been turned into a vast money laundering exercise for the friends in Palermo, and it acted as its pension fund.

Calogero must have known this, for why else would the Confraternity pay his mother five hundred euros a month? The six hundred members of the Confraternity were dupes, fools, people of unimpeachable respectability who were being used to shield the nefarious dealings of the friends in Palermo. Most of them had no idea, or they chose to have no idea. Petrocchi knew, because Petrocchi had guessed; occasionally, through intermediaries, one had the strange feeling that Palermo would be in touch if it so chose, that someone, someone in his office or elsewhere, was there, looking over his shoulder, making sure that he did not do anything that might endanger the interests of Palermo. Making sure, in short, that he asked no questions. They could always get in touch with you, if they so chose. But you were not supposed to get in touch with them.

The only way was to follow the money. On his return to the office, he had a sudden thought, and sent an email to one of the Confraternity accountants, a fairly lowly one, stating very simply: 'Calogero di Rienzi would like to consult with the benefactors who pay his mother's pension.' There was no reply. He had not expected one. In fact, the lack of a reply was a sign that his message had been understood. He found this disturbing. He had sent a simple message, but what had he unleashed? Perhaps, he felt glumly, a series of events that would culminate in his own death.

It was some weeks after the meeting in the Villa Bellini that Calogero got the message. He knew that he would be kept waiting, as the friends in Palermo would doubtless want to show that they were the important people, and that they could keep people waiting. A postcard was slipped under his door one night. It showed a picture of a snow-capped Mount Etna. Written on the card were the words 'The Lion roars this Sunday.' He understood the reference at once; and he wondered how the person who had delivered the card had managed to get into the building he lived in, through the normally locked street door. He very carefully destroyed the card, and then spoke to his wife, who was making his morning coffee.

'Have you ever seen the famous clock tower at Messina?' he asked.

'Never,' she replied.

'We can go on Sunday,' he said. 'My mother or yours can look after Isabella. And we can have lunch there.'

'A nice day out,' she said happily.

The lion would roar at noon. As a result, they took an early train that Sunday to Messina to be in the square outside the Cathedral in good time. Stefania had never witnessed the famous mechanical clock tower in Messina, and the things it did daily at noon. She was looking forward to it. At the same time, she was well aware that her husband was not the sort of man to take trips for no reason, and there was more to this than she imagined. Perhaps she was there to be a convenient alibi. Perhaps something was to happen in Catania at noon and Calogero needed to be in a crowded square with his wife some distance away to make sure that whatever happened in Catania could not be blamed on him. But perhaps, she reflected, she was his alibi in other ways as well.

They were in Messina in plenty of time, and they walked down the long street to the Cathedral square. Stefania, as was her habit, went into the Cathedral to follow the Mass; her husband stayed outside, found a bar, had coffee, and settled down to wait. As noon approached, as the people began to file out of the 11am Mass, the square began to fill up. People took their stand in front of the campanile to ensure a good view. The sunshine of autumn was pleasant. Just in time, as he was standing in the middle of the crowd, Stefania joined him. The bells began to toll. There were twelve distinct soundings of the great bell, then a pause. Then the machines inside the tower began to do what everyone came to see. Little men came out and went in again. Mechanical figures waved flags, moved artificial limbs with great awkwardness. It was not done well, but it was fascinating to see it done at all. Then the lion came out and there was a very load roar. At that precise moment, Calogero felt a movement as if someone were putting their hand uncomfortably close to his trousers. In fact, someone had done just that. He felt a slight shock at the sensation at the obtrusive unseen hand; but then he realised someone had placed a piece of paper in his back pocket. It was a very small piece of paper, but he could feel it all the same. But he was patient, and decided that he would not look at it until the crowd dispersed and he was alone.

The campanile returned to its usual serenity after lion roar and cock crow. Calogero and Stefania then moved to a restaurant nearby; they sat at a table, and ordered their food. Then Calogero excused himself to go to the bathroom. In one of the cubicles, he read the piece of paper. It was an address: a street, a number, an internal number to be rung; and a time. He memorised them, and then he flushed the piece of paper down the loo.

He rejoined his wife. They had barely spoken all day. They hardly ever spoke these days, except about their daughter, or money, or her cooking – purely practical matters. He wondered how she passed her time when he was not there, which was most of the time. He was conscious more than ever that they had not made love in a long time, despite the fact that they were only twenty years old; but that was the fault of Isabella, he told himself. He wanted another child, a boy, but perhaps it was best to wait. She knew he would never look at another woman.

'Did you enjoy the Mass?' he asked.

'Yes, it was very beautiful. The cathedral is very beautiful. I had no idea. They did a good job rebuilding it after the earthquake. The Mass was lovely. You should have come.'

'You went for both of us,' said Calogero. 'Did you pray for me?'

'Of course.'

'Thank you. That is kind of you. I do not deserve your kindness.' He leaned across the table and took her hand. This sort of display felt awkward. 'Don't look so surprised. I used to hold your hand a lot when you and I first met. That was nice. We were young. We are still young. Remember conceiving Isabella? What a delight that was. The night of the news of my father's death. Your parents were very understanding about me making their daughter pregnant. You were very understanding. But then times changed. I have lots of things to think about, lots of worries. I should be more domestically minded.'

This was as near he would ever get to an admission of inadequacy, she realised.

'I remember conceiving Isabella,' she said. 'I remember it very well. It is a pity you were not there for her birth. We called you, but you did not come. You were too busy beating up Ino and terrorising his parents.'

'What do you care about Ino?' he said. 'You did not know him. He was a drug dealer. He deserved it richly. But yes, you are right, I should have been there. I was there as soon as I was able to be there. I think I have said that before now.'

'As you say, you should learn to more domestic,' she remarked. ' You need to be more sweet tempered, more home loving, more family orientated. I am sure Rosario would have wanted you to be so. Too late for him now.'

She said this to needle him. Of course, it was not true, they both knew that. Everything he did, he did deliberately. Calogero had never lost his temper, with Rosario or anyone else. Calogero's violence was always planned. It was controlled, it was premeditated. That was why it frightened people, though, of course, it did not frighten her. She was the mother of his daughter, and of his future son, he hoped. He would never hurt her. Besides she had the capacity to hurt him, and he knew it. She was the alibi that could give him away at any moment and destroy him. His mother was of that generation, the generation that complied with their husband's every lie. She too would comply and did comply, but would exact a price for doing so.

'I didn't drive Rosario away,' he said defensively, conscious of this new domestic front opening up before him. 'It was Turiddu.'

'Nothing stirs without your permission,' she replied.

'Except, it seems, you,' he shot back. 'Turiddu acts the way he thinks I want him to act, but sometimes he may go a little far. Perhaps he went too far with Rosario. Did you speak to Rosario before he left? Are you in contact with him?'

'No. And I have not discussed it with don Giorgio. Let us just say this: your brother left for a reason. One can work out the reason. And it had something to do with Turiddu.'

'I didn't realise you took such an interest in Turiddu.'

That was a mistake.

'I don't,' she replied. 'You do.'

He would have tried to ignore this, but he felt his ears burn with embarrassment.

'Turiddu is a chatterbox. He has told people that you, yes, you, let him shit in his brother's mouth; that you were there when Turiddu threatened to cut off Rosario's balls with a knife. He has told people he can do what he likes, because you let him do what he likes. He has been screwing that prostitute from Romania and boasting about it.'

'Anna?'

'Is that her name?'

'That is her name,' said Calogero. 'And before you ask how I know her, she is my tenant. She rents two places. A room on the ground floor, where she works, and a room in the next street, at the top of a building, where she lives with her son. She is a good woman.'

Stefania raised an eyebrow.

'You will have seen her at Mass on Sundays. Her son, Traiano, made his first Holy Communion around the time we were married and is one of the altar boys, I believe.'

'And how does this living saint know someone like Turiddu?' she asked.

'I introduced them. The week before our wedding, when you were so busy having your dress fitted, it was Turiddu's thirteenth birthday, so I thought it was time he was made into a man. I took him one Sunday to Anna, when she was at home, and while I took the little boy out for an ice cream on the Via Etnea, which he greatly enjoyed, she took care of his needs.'

'Holy Mary,' said Stefania. 'Did the boy realise?'

'Traiano? He was too young then. He was about seven. He may do now. Anyway, so what?' said Calogero, cutting her off her objections. 'Turiddu still goes to see her. That is what boys do. He needs to prove himself.'

'To whom?'

'To himself, of course. Why are we talking about him?'

'You need to deal with him,' said Stefania. 'He is an embarrassment. To you. And to me.'

'I will deal with him. I will remind him who is boss. It won't be the first time. You don't need to worry about him. I will make sure he's respectful. And that he doesn't talk about Rosario or anything else.'

The waiter came with their first course. He looked at his spaghetti alle vongole with longing, as he picked up his fork.

'You do not understand what I am asking,' said Stefania. 'What I am telling you.'

'What are you telling me?' he asked.

'Kill Turiddu,' she said.

He carried on eating his pasta.

'Some things can be done at once, other things take time. You do not give the orders round here. I do. You need to trust me. And you need to be patient.' He took another mouthful. 'It is true that I have not been as attentive as I might. There have been things on my mind. And we have a young child, and I need my sleep at night, which is why I often spend time at my mother's or elsewhere. But I would like to have another child. And soon.'

She stared at him steadily and not kindly, then deliberately turned to her pasta.

'Look, Stefania,' he said, feeling his face burn, 'After Isabella was born, I gave you some time, I know that you wanted time, but you said, you made it clear...'

'What did I say? What did I make clear?' she asked.

'That you did not want it. That you were not interested in it; that you did not want me, you were not interested in me.' He paused, embarrassed, but having broached the subject at last, he determined to continue. It had to be said. 'Perhaps you don't like me that way. Perhaps you don't like me any way. Perhaps I am too rough, or too ugly, or just not affectionate enough. But let me tell you, Catania is full of affectionate people, and none of them can give you what I give you. Maybe I have some disadvantages, but in other ways... well, you went into this marriage with your eyes open. You wanted to marry me. I need a son. I have been very patient up to now.'

He boldly took her hand across the table. She laid her fork aside.

'Have you?' she asked, with no sympathy at all. 'Patient? Is that what you call it? You want a son, but you never come near me. You are at your mother's, or at Turiddu's, you sleep in the day, you stay up all night, you lock yourself away in your study and you look at your collection of filthy magazines. Yes, I know. Sometimes you forget to lock your desk. I would not be surprised if you had gone back to Anna.'

He was angry, but he kept his voice low.

'I am out because it is never worthwhile being in. You refused me.'

'I refused you, but I expected you to ask again, and again. But you took no for an answer. You fool.'

He was puzzled for a moment.

'Yes, but...' he began to reply, then he caught her uncompromising expression. 'Yes, you are right to be annoyed. Perhaps I should have been more insistent. Look. We will book the best hotel in Messina this afternoon, and go there, and then have dinner, and then spend the night, and then go back to Catania in the morning. You can phone your mother or my mother, so Isabella is looked after.'

This would be the first time they had spent the night outside Purgatory since their honeymoon. He called over the owner of the restaurant.

'My wife and I want to stay in the best hotel in the city. Can you recommend one? Could you take this?' he asked, taking out a credit card, 'and book their very best room for us?'

The man was all co-operation.

'Why are you using a card?' she asked. 'Why not cash? You never use a card.'

'True,' he said. 'I don't like them. But as the hotel is an unforeseen expense, I probably don't have enough cash. Just as well I brought the card. Even though I hardly ever use it.'

The man came back with the main course and with effusive details of the hotel he had booked in their name. Calogero was charm itself, and equally voluble in thanks. After the main course was over, Calogero paid the bill with the card, and engaged the man in more conversation. Stefania watched this, realising that he was preparing an excellent alibi for himself, and expecting to see the handsome and memorable tip. In due course a fifty euro note was flung carelessly on the table. The proprietor called a taxi for them, and as they were about to get into it, Calogero said:

'You go on ahead. I will join you as soon as I can.'

He ordered the driver to move before she could remonstrate. She watched him standing on the pavement as her car moved off. What had he come for? What was he going to do?

As she left him, he hurried off to his own rendezvous. The Via Garibaldi was not far away, and the number he had been given was that of a flat on the third floor of a perfectly anonymous building. The door buzzed at his ring, and a voice announced the third floor. Up he went, to find the door opened, and inside the flat, a man in a suit, of about sixty years of age. The man indicated a chair, sat down himself, and offered Calogero a cigarette, which he refused. He lit one. Calogero waited for him to speak.

'My name is Santucci, as I am sure you will have no difficulty finding out, if you should put your mind to it. Lorenzo Santucci. I knew your father, though I doubt he ever mentioned my name,' said the man at last. 'Nice man. Pity about his end. Pity about all that publicity. Most businesses love publicity, but not ours. We like discretion. Ever since then we have had you on our mind. We have discussed you. I have to tell you that some people thought you were a bit of a liability. Others said, no, let's wait and see. Some even thought you should be rubbed out for the crime of Via Vittorio Emanuele, but others thought your mother had had enough grief with the loss of her husband. And the murder of Vitale showed, what can I say, elan. Yes, spirit. And who was Vitale to us? A nobody. Utterly expendable. So we were not offended by his death; but we saw it for what it was – you showing off. Generally, we do not like show offs. Well, we have waited and seen. And now we have made a decision. We have listened, we have observed, we recognise that you have talent, and we now think that you can be of service to us.'

Calogero said nothing.

'We know that you are a thief, a very good thief in some ways, but not in others. We know that you have a hoard of stolen goods which you cannot offload. Well, we are going to help you. All those nice things that you have stolen with the help of your teenage accomplices and have still got – we know that you have still got them because they have not resurfaced anywhere – these things we will take and sell on for you, using our networks, our contacts. And you will get a fair price. Someone will be in touch to receive the stuff from you and to receive future things as well. The exception is the Spanish Madonna. That you give back. How is up to you. We want to keep the Confraternity on our side. We want to reward them for their co-operation. This man called Petrocchi is a respectable man, and useful to us. He wants the Madonna, has wanted her ever since you stole her, or so we have heard. So let him have it.'

'We know you are a whoremaster. Those dingy rooms full of dingy women. Catania needs an upgrade. We can provide you with personnel, from abroad, a higher quality; they will make more, you will make more, and part of the profit you can pass back to us. We only ask that you employ and house the people we supply, and you give us 20% of the rental income. We are not really interested in Catania, but, maybe one day that will change. Some of the better class girls can work that bar you own. And perhaps you could think of expanding into other bars. There is, as I am sure you know, always a market for whores, of the female kind and of the male kind.'

'We know you are a strong man, good with your fists, not frightened of anyone or anything. You like fighting, and you never lose a fight, perhaps because you are too calculating to enter a fight you could lose. There is someone in Catania who has displeased us. He is a drug dealer, with a little gang of helpers. I should speak carefully. He has not displeased us, he has displeased some of our friends in Catania, people you do not need to know about, not people on whose friendship we rely, but people who know people who can call in a favour. He has not shown the necessary deference. He needs to be removed from the scene. We tried to teach him a lesson, we tried to reason with him, but he seems intractable. His name is written here.'

The man passed Calogero a piece of paper. Calogero read it, and nodded. Then he put the piece of paper in his mouth, chewed it and swallowed it.

'You know of him? Good. No one will regret him in the least. It will be a nice opportunity for you to show us your skill. Do whatever you like, just make him disappear. Take your time with it, don't make any mistakes. He has a couple of thugs around him who will be eager to co-operate when he is gone. They will be no trouble at all to you or to us. Have you understood all this?'

'Yes,' said Calogero.

'Currently your mother receives 500 euro a month from the Confraternity. That is her pension as your father's widow. I will arrange for you to have a monthly stipend of 800 euros, payable to you, officially a pension for your father's four children. A lot of money is going to be coming your way. We pay you via the Confraternity; and you pay us the same way, whatever we ask.'

Santucci stood and held out his hand.

'How do I contact you?' asked Calogero.

'We contact you,' he said. 'Someone will be in touch about the stolen goods, about the whores. On the other matter, we rely on you. Do this well, and other jobs follow.'

The man left the flat without saying goodbye. Calogero sat down in the empty room, and reflected. He was one step further in.

Very soon he was in the street and making his way to the hotel where, he knew, his wife was waiting for him.

Later, before they went out to dinner, as he lay on the crumpled sheets in the hotel bedroom, and as he heard the water of the shower from the bathroom, he felt a sense of impending power and prosperity. Things were moving into a new phase. His wife, temporarily pacified, he hoped, was right about Turiddu. Whatever came next would not have Turiddu in it for long.

Chapter Six

At four in the morning Purgatory was deserted and the streets of the quarter empty. It was always so. It was, naturally enough, Calogero's favourite time, when he could walk the streets and survey them, think of the people asleep in the houses, and feel that he owned the place, and that there was no one to oppose him. Soon the blessing of Palermo would come, and then there would be no limit to what he would be able to control. For the moment, though, there were certain obstacles to be overcome.

Two streets away from his own house, he opened the street door to a familiar decayed building, and made his silent and dark way up the stairs to the top floor. Here too he opened the door with his landlord's key, and found himself in a single squalid room, freezing with the biting cold of midwinter, and, at the same time, fetid and stuffy. The room was divided by a flimsy partition (he remembered it from daylight visits) which squeaked as he pushed it aside. There were three people breathing in the room, he knew, distinguishing the sounds they made: one was a child; one was a woman; and the third was Turiddu, whose breathing as he slept was familiar to him. He took out a small torch and identified his quarry, saw the dirty blonde curly hair against the dirty grey pillow. He shone the torch at Turiddu's face and watched him stir. A moment later he prodded him. Turiddu awoke, and sensing who standing above him, was instantly alert. Calogero gestured him to get up, and to do so quietly, and to join him on the landing outside.

A moment later, Turiddu, hurriedly dressed in a pair of childish pyjamas, was there.

'You know who told me to look for you here?' said Calogero. 'My wife. Apparently, everyone knows about this, except me. I am the last to know.'

126

'Sorry, boss. I didn't think you would be interested in knowing. The women, they talk, you know. Anna will have talked and it will have worked its way all the way up to your wife.'

'Of course the women talk. They have nothing better to do. But it is you talking that worries me. Come here. Where did you get these pyjamas? Do they belong to her son? Good Lord. One day that boy will grow up and wonder what you were doing in his mother's bed, and decide to kill you.'

'He is only ten, boss.'

'Give him five years, then,' said Calogero grimly. There was a squashed packet of cigarettes and a lighter in the top pocket of the pyjamas. 'Go on, have one,' commanded Calogero. 'I have told you how I hate smoking. It is so bad for you. And it smells. But you smell already. You smell of her stale sheets. How many men has she had in her bed? What are you doing with her?'

'Nothing, we are just friends. I mean not nothing, but nothing much. I get into bed with her and she lets me hold her, and then I do it to myself, and then she lets me suck her tits and then we sleep.'

'You should cut your hair,' said Calogero, lifting the curls that covered the back of his neck. 'You might even think of washing it.'

He took the lit cigarette out of Turiddu's mouth. He applied its glowing tip to the skin at the back of his neck. The boy flinched. Calogero smiled.

'If you ever talk, I will torture you to death,' he said.

'Boss, I will never talk,' said Turiddu.

The burning end was applied once more to the back of his neck.

'How many people have you got buying the drugs?' asked Calogero casually.

'Seven or eight, boss, all regulars.'

'Good,' said Calogero. Turiddu flinched again, and this time he dug the cigarette deeper into his skin, until it was extinguished. Turiddu whimpered.

'Light another one,' said Calogero.

He watched the boy light another with trembling hands, the flame momentarily illuminating his thin sunken cheeks. Turiddu drew on the cigarette hungrily.

'What do you see in Anna?' he asked conversationally.

'We are friends, boss. She likes me, well, she likes the company. Either she is working or she is looking after the boy. Not much of a life. But you know her.'

'Yes, I do. I had her when I was thirteen. And I was the one who introduced you.'

'She is doing it for the boy. He is ten. The father is in Romania, and he does not know. But she sends money back to him. She has told him some story which he believes.'

'I bet he does. They all have some story, don't they? Perhaps we should find her a better job in due course. One day I am going to clear out all these whores and find better tenants, do these places up. But not just yet. I have a job for you.'

'Yes, boss?'

He was all attention.

'It demands the utmost secrecy.'

'Of course.'

'If you say a word to anyone, I will kill you. But before that I will kill your Anna and her son. Understood?'

'Have I ever talked?' asked Turiddu.

'God forbid that I should ever hear that you had. Tomorrow night I want you to go to a pizzeria near the airport. It is a large place on Viale Kennedy. There is a huge car park, a garden that people use in summer, and I think the pizza is good. At least I assume it is, as the place is packed with people. I have driven past it once or twice, and that is the impression I got. The man who owns it is a big noise. He has an office round the back.'

'You want me to rob him?'

'No, I just want you to go there and have a pizza – you can take Anna and Traiano, they will make you look unremarkable – go there as often as you like, become a regular. Get to know the place. This may be a long game we are playing. But you and I are going to kill the big noise. Though not just yet. We need to look for an opportunity, an occasion, and there is a complicating matter as well.'

'Are we going to make him disappear?' asked Turiddu.

'No. We very much want his body to be found by the police. You will have to wait and see why. The pizzeria is a front for his other business. I mean, it is a real pizzeria, but at the same time the big noise is a drug dealer. The stuff you are selling comes from him, through two or even three intermediaries. As you will see, the people going in and out doing deliveries are doing deliveries of more than just pizza. The pizzeria itself is a legal front for the illegal business.'

'Are we going to take it over?'

'Maybe. I might give it to you as a present. We shall see. Go there tonight.'

He took the cigarette off him, which was now almost smoked to the butt. Turridu awaited further pain, while his master lifted the curls and examined the back of his neck once more. The pattern, he observed, was pretty. The burns would heal after a few days. The others had all healed in a similar time. He threw away the stub, and put it out under his foot. Turiddu seemed relieved.

Calogero led the way back into the flat. Anna and the child had not stirred. He ran his torch over their sleeping faces. Presumably this sort of people spent most of the night awake, and most of their day asleep. His torchlight lingered for a moment, before he switched it off, and left on silent feet, closing the door quietly behind him.

Traiano, who was ten, could not believe their luck when he was told that Turiddu was taking them out for a pizza. And what a place, opposite the sea, with lots of waiters coming and going, all of whom made a huge fuss of the boy, as Sicilian waiters always did. The waiters also knew how to treat his mother too, calling her signora, making sure that she had their entire attention when they were with her. Anna looked her best. Rarely having a night off, she was happy and relaxed, especially as Turiddu was paying for everything, and had promised to make good any lost earnings. The waiters only had difficulty with Turiddu: was he her son? Was he her boyfriend? Was he some sort of relation? He was too old for one role, and too young for the other, though it was hard to discern just how old he was. He was puny, small, but muscular and strong. He looked unhealthy, with sunken eyes, and unwashed hair, a bit like an unloved child, or perhaps a drug abusing adult who had lost interest in looking after himself and fallen into the habit of self-neglect. Traiano, dressed in his best, looked bright enough; the darkness of the slums of Catania did not hang about him yet.

Anna knew that something was afoot, but she also knew not to ask questions. In fact she had given up wondering about strange things, she had renounced curiosity. The word why no longer entered her head. All she cared about was making enough money and looking after her child, whom she had brought to Italy to get away from her abusive husband, who was bribed to stay away by a monthly remittance. In her trade one met all sorts of strange behaviour, and eventually one did not wish to know any more than one had to about men and their inexplicable ways. Let the unexplained, and possibly inexplicable, remain so, she thought. Live for the moment. Observe, and say nothing.

The room was vast, and pizza poured out of the kitchen at a steady rate. It was a noisy room too, and the waiters shouted one to another. She noticed how Turiddu's eyes travelled around the room, watching the waiters bring the pizza, take away plates, carry trays high with drinks. There was also a steady stream of pizza in boxes leaving the restaurant, carried away by boys in motorcycle gear, each with the restaurant's name on the back of their jackets. Each rider carried about ten large pizza boxes which were fitted into large containers on the back of their bikes. These, he saw at once, were the drug couriers. Just a table away, a large party of uniformed police were eating and drinking. He noticed that they were not presented with a bill. Before they left, someone came out from the back of the restaurant, and shook them all by the hand and assured them that they were always welcome and looked forward to seeing them again. This was the owner, the big noise. His name was Carmine del Monaco. Turiddu watched him covertly. He was about fifty years old, strong and well built, physically fit, smartly dressed, with hair well slicked back – a man who was successful and pleased with himself. Turiddu immediately felt the desire to kill him. It would be nice, not just to level, but to utterly destroy such a huge ego as he felt sure Carmine del Monaco possessed. The only question was how? There were so many people around in the pizzeria, that while one could get to him, one could not reasonably hope to get away. But there again, one could simply stab the man and walk away; by the time people realised what was wrong, you would be long gone, and if one did it carefully, no one would notice anything amiss for a few vital seconds, by which time their minds would be so befuddled by shock that they would not remember anything important.

Carmine del Monaco was now returning to the office at the back of the premises, and stopping at different tables to say hello to various people, as befitted the big noise he was. Turiddu saw it: a very sharp knife straight into the guts and twisted as he passed the table; then the look of surprise on his face, rapidly succeeded by the horror of the sight of his own blood spurting out and covering the floor. Oh what a fine sight that would be!

He could see it all. The pizzeria had large linen table napkins which would be excellent for holding and hiding the knife, which, when inserted into the guts of del Monaco could be left exactly where it was. He would tell Calogero all about this, and how happy the boss would be.

As soon as Carmine del Monaco was through the door out of the restaurant and into his office at the back, his face changed. The smile vanished, the goodwill evaporated. He cursed the policemen and women who had just been eating for free and drinking at his expense. He had been paying them off for years; each man and woman in the local force was on some kind of retainer, and each of them was salivating at the prospect of getting more. After all, his business was growing, the money was coming in, their co-operation was necessary (or at least their turning of a blind eye) so why shouldn't they get more if he were getting more? That was their reasoning. He himself did not see it that way. He resented the way everyone, but everyone, wanted him to give them money: his wife, his children, his employees, the couriers, everyone who worked for him, they had but one refrain: please give us more. His turnover was enormous, but he felt he had continually to guard his fortune from the scavengers and scroungers who circled him.

Of course, he was prospering, it was undeniable. The pizzeria dealt, naturally enough, in pizza, and was always full of people. The men who made the pizza were the one group he was never unwilling to pay more. The boys who went out on scooters to deliver pizza, also delivered other things to a network of dealers around the city. These dealers brough their cash back to the pizzeria, and the restaurant 'washed' their money; in recent times the money was so good, that del Monaco had bought several bars and a couple of other pizzerias as well, to help with the laundering of dirty money. He was fifty-two and he was rich. God had been good to him.

As for the local police, he had taken what he thought everyone would see as a reasonable line with them. He had given them a raise all round, though not quite the raise they had asked for. He knew, and surely they should as well, that when you made a demand, you should always settle for less. He had given them half of what they had asked for, which had cost him a considerable amount, and expected them, if not to be grateful, then at least to shut up for a few years. It had worked. They had taken the cash and stopped moaning. They had perhaps realised that when you see a source of money you should not get too greedy, you should not drink the well dry all at one go.

But there had been one exception. One of the younger men had not had the sense to understand this. He had complained that the settlement was not generous enough. This had infuriated Carmine del Monaco; here he was, being generous, letting everyone have what they deserved, letting everyone profit from his hard work, and this one little bastard had made difficulty. He obviously needed to learn a lesson of respect to his elders and to the way things had been done up to now and would always be done.

Not only had this cop, a man called Fabrizio Perraino, failed to shut up, he had decided to make trouble. He was a smooth faced young man with the good looks of a movie star, a poseur, and he had taken to stopping and search the boys who delivered the pizza. On one occasion he had stopped and searched a boy who was carrying something other than pizza and arrested him. That had proved awkward. The delivery boy had of course refused to speak, had said nothing at all, and refused to answer any questions. Carmine del Monaco had sent one of his understrappers, the one called Alberto, down to the station to explain what was what. The police were very understanding, indeed embarrassed by the overenthusiasm of their colleague Fabrizio, and were happy to let the boy go with a warning; but Fabrizio Perraino, damn him, had suggested that charges be pressed. Alberto was insistent that this would cause a great deal of trouble to the boy, his parents and above all to Carmine del Monaco. But Fabrizio Perraino had just smiled that infuriating bland smile.

Alberto had gone away and reported back, whereupon Carmine had sent down his other assistant, the one called Alfredo, with an envelope containing one thousand euro. Carmine did not like giving into blackmail in this way, but it seemed the easiest way for the moment. He did not want the pizza delivery boy to get a criminal record. It seemed to be the best thing to do, for the moment. Perraino took the money, and let the delivery boy go.

A couple of weeks later, Perraino was set upon by Alfredo and Alberto when out in the street one Sunday afternoon. He was bundled into a car, and brought, terrified, for an interview with Carmine del Monaco. In the back room of the pizzeria, Carmine broke Perraino's jaw in three places; then Alberto and Alfredo drove the man out into the countryside and dumped him. After this, Carmine had expected there would be no more trouble, and the police, and Perraino in particular, would learn their lesson.

In fact while some of the older and more experienced members of the force thought that Perraino had been very stupid and got what was coming to him, and was a warning to everyone else, a few, mainly younger colleagues, were appalled and angered by the incident. The sight of Perraino, formerly so handsome, with his face bruised and his jaw wired up, lying in his hospital bed, alerted them to what they had known all along: that Carmine del Monaco was a criminal and a brute with no respect for the law, and no respect for the police. There was a demand made that del Monaco should be arrested and his pizzeria closed down as a crime scene.

Carmine del Monaco was not in the least bit worried that this would come to pass, that he would be arrested for assault, and put on trial. Who would dare testify against him, apart from Perraino? And if he were ever in the witness box, he could certainly drag many of them down with him. They were all complicit, they were all guilty. His assault on Perraino had been carefully predicated on this impunity that he enjoyed. He knew they would all calm down and that the message would get through, namely that the old way of doing things was the best way of doing things.

Much to his annoyance, though, and to the annoyance of many of the police themselves, the matter refused to die. Signora Perraino, seeing her son lying in his hospital bed, refused to leave the matter alone. She visited his superiors, who felt they had to see her, and demanded action. This was unusual, as women generally knew that they should keep out of men's quarrels. It was explained to her as gently as possible that her precious son had only himself to blame for his predicament. But she refused to accept this. Eventually, they shut their doors against her and refused to see her. A message came to Carmine that the woman was being difficult, but that was not their fault. They had not encouraged her.

Carmine del Monaco was annoyed by this astonishing lack of stoicism on the woman's part. She ought to have been grateful for not seeing her son lying in his coffin. That is what he said to her when she came to confront him and to make a scene in his office. Signora Perraino was in her mid-forties and quite a sexy thing, or so Carmine thought, as she screamed and shouted at him. But he had eventually lost patience with her, and had to explain to her how things worked, something that neither she nor her son seemed to grasp. Before throwing her out of his office, and warning her never to come back and never to annoy him again, he had told her to stop complaining or something worse would happen to her and her son. Yes, he had made a few threats. In fact, one very specific threat. He had told her that he would get his two deputies, Alfredo and Alberto, to rape her. And he would rape her himself. Given that she was a good-looking woman (he had always liked the mature type) he thought this an amusing threat, an agreeable prospect.

'You have insulted me,' said the woman. She turned to Alberto and Alfredo. 'You are witnesses.'

And very quietly, she left.

Carmine shrugged it off, despite what he knew about offended women never giving up a fight, but seeking revenge for years and years. But he was not bothered by her. He was Carmine del Monaco, after all, and who was she? But Alberto and Alfredo, who had witnessed the incident, were not happy about it. Rape was a terrible crime in their eyes. It was something you associated with foreigners. They themselves were strict one-woman men. They had both been with their wives since their teenage years. They were domestic creatures. They believed in family. Rapists, to their mind, should be shown no mercy, but should be killed. (Indeed, Alberto and Alfredo were great believers in the death penalty, thinking it the only answer to most of the misdemeanours of which they disapproved.) Threatening to rape the mother of a foolish man like the young policeman crossed a boundary. The signora had been insulted. She was right about that. Carmine had wronged her. They hesitated about what to do. First, without telling Carmine, they sent a message to the signora to placate her, to make clear that they were not responsible for the insult, and they did not share in it. But that was a mistake. Realising that there was a fissure between del Monaco and his closest deputies, the signora, intent on revenge, decided to take the train to Palermo.

137

At this point, Alfred and Alberto, who were brothers, panicked. If she were going to Palermo, as she threatened, hinting that she had connections, and that her sister, Fabrizio's aunt, who was very fond of him, was very well connected, then it was necessary that they call Palermo and got in their side of the story beforehand. This they did, after some difficulty. And so it turned out that the signora, when she had lunch in Palermo with an old friend who remembered the days of her great beauty, an old friend moreover who was friends with friends who had influence, this old friend knew everything about the case. Alfredo and Alberto were told not to worry, to do nothing, to stand by, to wait.

To wait for what was not quite clear to them. But they waited, tense, expecting something to happen. And nothing did. There was a pause. Business went on as usual. People came, and people went. Then one day a contact from Palermo arrived. They were not present when this messenger called, but they heard about the substance of it from their boss.

Palermo had heard the lady's complaint and upheld it. They had pointed out to Carmine that he should not have assaulted Fabrizio Perraino so viciously. Assaulting the police was always more trouble than it was worth. There were better ways of dealing with young fools such as Perraino, such as, for example, talking to their superior officers, wise men who understood the way things worked. In the eyes of Palermo, he had stepped over the boundary with Perraino, and done the same with the mother. The mother was someone, and her sister, Anna Maria Tancredi, was an important banker in the world of Palermo. There were certain people it was best never to offend. He ought to compensate both son and mother, in order to preserve the peace, by paying a hundred thousand euros to the policeman and twenty thousand to the mother.

Carmine raged and shouted and swore. He swore he would drive to the hospital and finish off the job, by killing Fabrizio Perraino in his bed. He would then drive to wherever the mother lived and rape and kill her. He raged at mother and son; and he raged at Palermo. How dare they treat him like this?

But the truth was that he was only allowed to operate his very successful business because Palermo allowed him to do so. It was not simply that they granted permission for him to do as he pleased in his part of Catania; they also were his suppliers. Not a gram of cocaine moved in the island without them knowing of it and approving it. So, his fury was in vain. There was only one possible course of action, and that was to go to Palermo, to speak to the people in charge, and put his case, and appeal against the sentence. He did not care too much about the money: it was the principle of the matter that concerned him. Palermo should back him, not Fabrizio Perraino and his mother.

And so he went to Palermo, and had a meeting in the bar of the Grand Hotel. It was brief and unsatisfactory. The man he saw, who was called Antonio Santucci, spoke with the authority of the people at the top, he assured him, and over negronis told him what the situation was. He, Carmine del Monaco, had severely messed things up in the eyes of Palermo. Indeed, Palermo was furious. A fine of 120,000 euros was mild. He should consider himself lucky. The truth was, as far as Palermo was concerned, that the police had to be kept onside at all times. Assaulting the police hardly ever paid, and if it were to be undertaken, clearance should be sought first. Moreover, things were complicated by the aunt, Anna Maria Tancredi, who had been extremely fond of her once handsome nephew. Her goodwill was vital to their interests. As it was, Carmine should have reined in his anger and supressed his temper.

It was exactly this that he then failed to do. Keeping his voice low, he cursed the woman and her son, and he cursed the aunt, and he cursed Palermo. They had no idea. All his hard work in Catania – what did they know about that? After Carmine stormed out, Antonio Santucci carried on sipping his negroni, and then asked for the bill. He knew that his father and his uncle would not be pleased. Indeed, the next day it was clear to them that, though the money was paid as requested, there was a Catania problem. This was discretely communicated to Alberto and Alfredo.

Because he had paid, though under protest, Carmine thought the matter closed. Alberto and Alfredo thought differently. They awaited the inevitable change of management. They were filled with foreboding and anticipation. For who, after all, would take over, if not themselves? They had always got on well with Carmine, but he had clearly lost the use of his reason. And so they waited. On the other side of the city, in Purgatory, Calogero was waiting too – for the day of the murder.

The day came. Saturday evening was always the busiest evening in every pizzeria, and the evening on which the traffic in Catania was at its most solid, particularly along the Viale Kennedy. The first step was the theft of the motorcycle and the special jacket that the delivery boys wore. On Friday evening late, as he discretely surveyed the carpark, Turiddu selected his victim, purely on the grounds of size and hair colour. On his own (stolen) motorbike, he followed this boy on his errand, and as he stopped outside a block of flats, he approached him, wearing his helmet with the visor down. As the boy attempted to open the pizza box at the back of the bike, Turiddu approached with a knife, which he held against the boy's trembling flesh. Terrified, the boy backed away, and, when told to do so, surrendered his jacket. Of course he realised at once that he would be in huge trouble with the pizzeria for losing the bike; but he also knew that the bike and the jacket were going to be used in a crime, and that the trouble of losing the bike would be nothing compared to the trouble he would cause himself if he were to report the bike stolen. But if he were to say nothing, and later it emerged, as it surely would, that he had lost the bike? An insurance policy was called for. He called Alberto, to tell him what had happened. Alberto was the one to whom he had been instructed to turn if there were ever problems. The boy was convinced that the theft was the work of some other drug network, but Alberto was thoughtful but reassuring.

'Never mind,' he said. 'We will sort it out. Take tomorrow off. You will be paid. I will ask around and get you the bike back by Sunday at the latest.'

The crime was committed just after 8pm on a Saturday night in March. Turiddu waited in the dark of the car park, looking through the brightly lit windows of the pizzeria, waiting to see when Carmine del Monaco would emerge into the restaurant and greet people at various tables, something that he invariably did at about this time. As soon as he saw the man appear, he stepped out into the light for a moment. He knew that at the other end of the car park Calogero was waiting for this signal.

Calogero was in a van that he had stolen that same morning, a perfectly ordinary van. He now went round to the back, opened it, and took out the painting of the Spanish Madonna, which was covered with a sheet and not too large for one man to handle. He carried it round to the back of the pizzeria, and banged on the door loudly. After a moment's hesitation, which was sure sign that visitors were not expected, the door was opened by Alberto, with Alfredo looking on in the background.

'Special delivery from Palermo,' explained Calogero. 'Where do you want it?'

They understood at least something. The word 'Palermo' was a word they had been expecting to hear. They stood aside while Calogero, panting slightly, put the painting, still covered, against the only free wall in the office.

'Advise you not to touch it,' he said, and quickly left them.

'Who was that?' asked Alfredo.

'No idea,' said Alberto.

He lifted the sheet. They both gazed at the painting which was lying on its side. Turning their heads, they examined it, and the recognised it.

'Holy Mary,' said Alfredo.

'Mother of God,' said Alberto, crossing himself.

At that very moment, the restaurant, always noisy, became suddenly silent, then turned to uproar, a cacophony of men shouting, women screaming and children crying. The two looked at each other, but neither moved.

He had waited long enough for the boss to get in the back and deliver the picture, then saying a little prayer for success, Turiddu strode into the restaurant with a confidence he did not entirely feel. But confidence alone was what one needed to pull off a job like this. He held the knife in his hand, concealed in a napkin. He saw Carmine del Monaco directly in front of him, large, convivial, laughing, deep in conversation with a table of clients. He was leaning slightly forward. Turiddu, without a moment's hesitation, plunged the knife into the small of his back, straight into one of his kidneys. Del Monaco turned with a look a mild surprise as if someone had had the effrontery to bump into him. His eyes looked at Turiddu in puzzlement and contempt, and in a new sensation that was suddenly upon him, pain. Turiddu now plunged the knife into the man's stomach, drawing it across him to make as large a cut as possible. He saw horror in del Monaco's face.

'Jesus', said Del Monaco, looking down, seeing his blood, clutching himself, seeing his guts spill.

There was a sudden silence, and through this silence Turiddu turned and walked out. The whole room seemed for a moment frozen in puzzlement, echoing the sensations of del Monaco himself who was now beyond sensation. As Turiddu reached the door there were the beginnings of uproar. By the time he had put on the motorcycle helmet, he could hear the pandemonium behind him. But a few seconds after that, though it seemed longer, he was riding south through the traffic on the Viale Kennedy. After not very long, leaving the degraded suburbs behind him, he came to the deserted stretch of beach that he had visited earlier. Here he disposed of the bike by the simple expedient of pushing it into the sea; then he found the bag he had hidden earlier. He stripped naked, jumped into the freezing sea himself to wash for a moment, then dressed himself in the new clothes in the bag. The old clothes and the bag he disposed of by throwing them into the sea as well. Then he turned back to the road, and began the long walk back to the Viale Kennedy, from where, having disposed of the stolen van, Calogero had arranged to pick him up.

Within twenty minutes they were both entering the bar in the square outside the Church of the Holy Souls in Purgatory; and when the television set began a live transmission from the pizzeria on Viale Kennedy, they looked as surprised as anyone else. 'Horror in the Pizzeria,' announced the strapline. It made, for a variety of reasons, compulsive viewing.

Everyone in the pizzeria had had a mobile phone, and everyone used them immediately the crime was committed. Some with the most advanced models even used their phones to film the spectacle of Carmine del Monaco lying on the floor of his own restaurant in a pool of blood. The police arrived rapidly, and when it was clear that nothing could be done for the dead man, cleared the restaurant and did their best to seal it off. The clientele, some of whom wisely took their uneaten pizza with them, were corralled in the carpark, while the police took their details, and while the camera crew and reporters from RAI tried their very best to get the first interviews from eye-witnesses. The restaurant was large and had been very busy. There had been over two hundred people inside and a queue of people waiting outside. There was no shortage of people wanting to give their account of what had happened.

'What a mess,' said Turiddu as he and Calogero were watching the television in the bar.

Calogero nodded.

'All those people,' said Calogero, not taking his eyes off the screen. 'There will be no forensic evidence at all. These clowns,' he added, meaning the police, 'have let a herd of cattle stampede over a crime scene. Whoever did this will get away with it.'

Everyone in the bar nodded.

They kept on watching for another hour. Turiddu became fidgety and bored, but he could see that the boss wanted to keep on watching. And in the end the wait was worth it. The cameras revealed two smiling policemen standing either side of the Spanish Madonna in Carmine del

Monaco's office, in exactly the same place where Calogero had left her a few hours earlier. The gasp in the bar was audible.

Within minutes, the quarter was alive. Women hung out of their windows shouting the news. People stood on their balconies and applauded. Children, woken from sleep, jumped up and down with glee.

'The kidnapped Madonna has been liberated,' was the cry heard throughout Purgatory.

Don Giorgio opened the Church of the Holy Souls in Purgatory. He switched on all the lights. Then he began to ring the bells.

In the bar, Calogero, who owned the place, ordered a bottle of prosecco for himself and free drinks for everyone.

Within half an hour, a camera crew from RAI turned up. Don Giorgio was interviewed.

He was moved to quote scripture: 'For lo, the winter is past, the rain is over and gone. The flowers appear on the earth; the time of the singing of birds is come. Tomorrow we shall have a Te Deum. As you can see, we are all very happy. Our quarter has had a lot of bad luck, ever since the Madonna was kidnapped. But now, they will bring her home and all will be well.'

The RAI crew filmed the interior of the Church, where several women were prostrate in thanksgiving before the high altar.

In the bar they interviewed a handsome confident man who was drinking prosecco.

'I was baptised in front of the Madonna, and I wished that my daughter had been baptised in front of her too. I was born and bred in Purgatory, and so she is my second mother. I just hope the police bring her back as soon as possible,' said Calogero.

By this time, the Archbishop of Catania, who had been watching the evening news in his residence, decided to get on the television rather than just watch it. By now all the bells of the city were ringing.

'The return of the Madonna,' said His Grace, from the steps in front of the Church of the Holy Souls in Purgatory, 'is a blessing for the people of this quarter and to the whole city. This is a moment of profound joy, and, I hope, spiritual renewal. It is not just that a great work of art has been recovered. The Mother of us all is coming home. I have spoken to the Police Commissioner and told him that she needs to be here tomorrow evening. And he agreed. Our Blessed Mother is returning to her beloved children.'

It was observed that several people standing round the Archbishop were in tears as he said this.

The lawyer Petrocchi also arrived, and surveyed the scene. He too managed to get himself on the television; after all, if credit and publicity were going for free, he wanted his share. And he was the one who was the author of all this joy.

Later, he went into the bar and saw Calogero.

'Congratulations,' he said.

It was two in the morning by the time the quarter quietened down, the bar closed, the bells stopped ringing and everyone went to bed.

Calogero and Turiddu stood in the deserted square.

'My wife is waiting for me,' said Calogero, looking up at the place where he lived, noting that the bedroom light was still on. 'I have to keep her happy. I must not keep her waiting too long. You have done well.'

'So have you, boss.'

'I am going to give you 20,000; I was going to give you ten, but I feel particularly generous tonight.'

'Thanks, boss. I would have done it for nothing. I really enjoyed myself.'

'You work for love not money. All the best workers do,' said Calogero.

'You know I do,' said Turiddu.

Calogero looked up at the window once more.

'How would you like the money? In cash? Or you want something like a car?'

'Boss, I would like one of the better flats for Anna, rent free for however long you want to give it to me. So she can live a bit better, you know?'

Calogero nodded.

'That's a good choice,' he said. 'Consider it arranged. I will see what we have available or what can be made available. You can go and tell her. Good night. Sleep well. Until tomorrow.'

They parted.

Turiddu made his way to the place where Anna lived. The child was asleep behind the partition, but to his surprise she was awake and, it seemed, waiting for him.

'That man has been killed, you heard? At that very pizzeria you took us to. How strange,' she said to him.

He undressed and got into bed with her.

'It is very strange,' he agreed, putting his arms around her, and burying his face in her ample bosom.

'And now the Madonna will come back, and everything will be better,' she said. 'You will see.'

She was not usually this talkative.

'Everything will be better,' echoed Turiddu. 'As a matter of fact, everything is already better. Much better than you think. Calogero is giving me a flat. A big flat with room for you and Traiano too. This may be your last night here.'

'What? Why?' she asked.

'I asked him. He likes me. That's all. I asked him, and he was in a good mood. So, we are getting a flat.'

'Thank you, Mother of God,' said Anna.

'Thank Calogero, thank me; but you can thank her too,' he said.

He snuggled down into her bosom once more.

'You won't have to work anymore,' he said sleepily. 'One day soon, we should try making a baby.'

'Thank you, darling,' she said happily, and she felt him drift off to sleep.

In the flat overlooking the square, Stefania said:

'The Madonna will send us a son, and soon.'

'I have tried my best to help,' said Calogero. 'Tomorrow will be a great day.'

The next day the two stories, really one story, continued to command the attention of the city. The first was the recovery of the Spanish Madonna. The second was murder of Carmine del Monaco. The press, the television, aided by the police, were adamant that the presence of the picture and the murdered man in the same place was no coincidence. Del Monaco had been murdered because of the picture. The picture had got him killed. But just how, that was hard to say. The connection between the two was not clear.

For the superstitious and the religious, the story was simple. Carmine del Monaco had kidnapped their Madonna, and the result was that misfortune had befallen him. Woe to all who despoiled churches, and to all impious hands that touched the sacred.

The police, of course, had wanted to take the Madonna into custody, saying that the picture was evidence. But the Archbishop of Catania himself had made sure that any bureaucratic delay had to be overcome and the picture had to be returned to its shrine the very next day. And so it was arranged, after much shouting at the Police Commissioner down the phone. A police escort would bring the painting back to the Church of the Holy Souls in Purgatory for 5pm. Moreover, His Grace the Archbishop would be there to receive the sequestrated Madonna, and then celebrate High Mass and lead the Te Deum of thanksgiving. His Grace had spent his entire life in the shadow of the man who was now Cardinal Archbishop of Palermo. They had been at school together and at seminary together. Now was the moment for Catania, namely himself, to overshadow the Cardinal. His Eminence had been on the phone from Palermo but His Grace had been unable to take the call. The last thing the Archbishop wanted was for the Cardinal to come from Palermo and steal his limelight. Though, in fairness, he was not an egotist. While he made sure he reported the news to the Pope, and had a precious three minutes on the phone with the Holy Father (who in truth, though they had met several times, never quite seemed to know who he was, and this time was no different), he was quite willing to share his glory, or rather the Madonna's glory, with the police who had liberated her, and with the head of the Confraternity, the lawyer Petrocchi, and even with don Giorgio (someone he had known for decades, but always had difficulty placing.)

To be kind to a priest as unimportant as don Giorgio would be seen as an act of great graciousness. Indeed, he might make him a canon of the Cathedral, or perhaps a Monsignor. That would be a nice idea, and the people would like it. (However, no sooner had the nice idea entered his head, then it faded away.) As for the lawyer Petrocchi, and the Confraternity, these were people worth cultivating too. One always wanted to have princes and dukes around one for effect, as it threw into relief one's concern for the poor and the marginalised. As for Petrocchi, he was clever and very rich; the Confraternity had money which he controlled; huge benefactions flowed from those coffers; Petrocchi's wife gave the most splendid parties at which the food and the wine were superb. They had a villa on the slopes of Mount Etna, with a lovely pool and they had a boat as well. It was all very well living next to the Cathedral and enjoying the fabulous view, but sometimes one longed for the softer things in life.

The return of the Madonna was to be broadcast by RAI to the whole peninsula. There were hastily assembled panels of experts to discuss the

151

event. Obscure priests who taught in seminaries were there to talk about the significance of the honour paid to the Madonna; a few alarmed experts on Velasquez were dragged out of hiding to stand in front of the cameras like rabbits caught in headlights. Petrocchi was there to talk about the Confraternity. Several important authors were there to talk about the way criminals had recently found their way into the art world, and how the recovery of this painting was well-nigh miraculous. Some hitherto neglected historians were on hand to talk about the Purgatory quarter of Palermo and its Church of the Holy Souls. Numerous experts were there to speculate on who had killed Carmine del Monaco and why he had had the painting in the first place.

The Archbishop, a short fat man, looked magnificent in his lace alb and embroidered chasuble. He conceded a plenary indulgence to all who prayed before the Madonna's shrine. The painting was put back in place to general applause. After the Mass was over, for hours afterwards, a long and patient queue of people – not something you often saw in Sicily – waited for their chance to see the Madonna in her rightful place, amidst her own people, after her Babylonian exile. The atmosphere, for several days, was ecstatic. Candles burned, and the Church of the Holy Souls in Purgatory stayed open all night. It was confidently averred that peace, prosperity and all good things would now return to the quarter with its Protectress.

As she had predicted, Stefania did become pregnant on the night of the del Monaco murder; the child, whom Calogero was convinced would be a boy, turned out to be another girl, however. As she was born so close to Christmas, she was called Natalia.

Chapter Seven

The friends in Palermo were very pleased by the removal of Carmine del Monaco from the scene. When they encountered each other by chance in the lobby of the Grand Hotel, or passed each other on the Via Maqueda, they nodded to each other with a reserve which was tempered by a pleasant sense of triumph. Carmine del Monaco was a problem who had been solved and who now no longer existed. He would serve only as a warning to others. And what had he been, except a common criminal with thoughts and ambitions above his station? Such men deserved to be cut down. There was no sin greater than the sin of pride; and there was no annoyance greater than someone who would not obey the rules, and who would not keep things running smoothly. This new man in Catania was young, respectful and above all sensible, something that Carmine del Monaco, God rest him, had never really been. The new man had a sense of deference; they could do business with him.

The police in Catania were, by contrast, deeply perturbed by the murder of Carmine del Monaco. It was a terrible embarrassment: the murder of a man in his own restaurant before numerous witnesses, and no one had seen anything, and there was no forensic evidence at all either. This sort of murder was not something they had to deal with very often. Clearly del Monaco had had enemies, which was disturbing, for they did not like the idea of the friends settling their accounts in this violent, indeed spectacular, manner. Of course, they knew what Carmine's business had been. Everyone had known, though everyone had, at the same time, pretended not to know. This arrangement had seemed to work very well, and now it was all up in the air. These changes were never good, unless change was carefully managed. Moreover, there was a double pressure on the police. First, they had to find the killer, something that seemed well-nigh impossible; and second, they had to avoid giving ammunition to their critics and looking like a bunch of incompetents. In this case, that seemed impossible as well.

One fear was that there might be an all-out gang war in Catania, something that there had never been up till now. If there were, it would be disastrous for everyone, and the first casualty in such a war would be the myth that Catania had no gangs and no organised crime. The revelation that it did would shatter any reputation for competence the police might have had; but it would also be deeply damaging to the gangs themselves, whose greatest advantage was the general denial that they existed.

But no one at all rose up to avenge the slaughtered Carmine del Monaco; his two deputies, Alberto and Alfredo, were only too happy to see him gone and to take over his business, so that everything might continue exactly as before. The friends in Palermo certainly wanted it that way, as did the police, who were in awe of their political masters, who in their turn refused to countenance the idea that Catania had a drug problem.

The handling of the news was relatively easy. A respected businessman, owner of one of the most popular pizzerias in the city, and other outlets besides, had been killed and in the process been revealed as a handler of stolen goods, in this case the Spanish Madonna of Velasquez. The Madonna herself had come down from her place in heaven to punish him – that was the way the popular mind worked. Or in other terms, the man was killed because he had failed to hand the Madonna over to its buyers, or attempted to cheat them in some way, and the murderers had been disturbed in their work and fled without the painting. This unlikely story was given a veneer of plausibility because the police had arrived at the scene when the body was still warm and leaking blood and life hardly extinct. The early arrival of the police had prevented the murderer and his accomplices getting hold of the painting.

Alfredo and Alberto had on the very night of the killing driven to Palermo to seek an audience with the friends first thing the next morning. They had been kept waiting for a few nerve-wracking days, during which time they had constantly looked over their shoulders, consoling themselves with the melancholy thought that if the friends had decided to take them out as well, then they would already have done so. They were haunted by the scene of Carmine lying in a pool of his own blood, with his guts spilled out on the marble flooring. Of course, they had seen similar sights in the past, but nothing that had touched them so nearly. It was imperative that they made their case, their excuses, to the friends, that they cleared themselves once more, that they convinced them that Carmine's fault was Carmine's fault alone, not theirs. Meanwhile the pizzeria remained shut, for reasons of bereavement, as was customary. And the drug-users of the southern part of the city's suburbs found themselves out of supply.

Eventually the two brothers were granted the interview they sought. Things were settled. Carmine, God rest him, was out of the picture. He had been foolish. He had not listened to reason. He had overstepped the mark. This happened from time to time. But now Alfredo and Alberto could take over the business; they could reopen the pizzeria. The widow would get her cut, and they would make sure she did. In return she would not distract them in any way. The whole business was theirs. Well, almost. One important adjustment needed to be made. Calogero needed a cut of the action. Every week they would send him a certain amount of stuff for him to sell. He would send one of his boys to collect it. Alfredo and Alberto bowed their heads on hearing this. They would go along with the new arrangement. It was what the friends wanted. They knew what happened to those who displeased the friends.

They themselves would not see Calogero. They were relieved by this. The thought of seeing the man who had delivered the painting just as Carmine was being murdered in the next room worried them. Instead they would see whatever boy Calogero sent. Before the murder they had never heard of this Calogero. But now, they saw he had the confidence of the friends, and they respected him. Which meant that they feared him.

It was shortly after the murder of Carmine del Monaco that Fabio Volta, the policemen who had investigated the death of the Chemist and the death of Vitale, his supplier, was transferred from Catania at his own request, to take a up a new position in Rome. He had decided that he ought to leave Catania because the sense of despair that he felt was too much for him, and to remain in the city and on the force in the city would be to have almost daily reminders of the way he had failed to tackle the canker at the heart of the city's life. The murder of Carmine del Monaco, and the fact that the killer would never be found, was the last straw. The investigation had been badly handled form the start, the crime scene barely secured, and he feared that the police themselves had had some involvement in it. Clearly, such a public murder had to have the blessing of the friends in Palermo, and it was well known that del Monaco had assaulted Fabrizio Perraino and broken his jaw in three places. Had Perraino called in the powers from Palermo? And who acted for the men from the Grand Hotel in Catania? The liberation of the picture was the obvious clue. He saw in this the man who had killed, he was sure, Vitale – Calogero di Rienzi.

He was certain of this, and equally certain that any investigation would be most unwelcome: it would disturb too many vested interests. He sensed, for this reason, that his career in the city of his birth was blocked, and that people were desperate for him to move northwards and to take up less contentious work. He was given to understand that his investigations, if left unchecked, would get them all killed, and so it was better that he stopped investigating altogether. As a result, he found himself in Rome. He had always wanted to be in Rome, and somewhat to his surprise, a job in Rome was offered. It was as if they could not wait to get rid of him, and wanted to ease his passage out of Catania. But the job in Rome turned out to be a snare and a delusion. He found himself chained to a desk, involved in the most banal administrative work.

The person who came to his rescue was his old colleague, now retired, Storace. They met occasionally for lunch, and Storace, who had spent his whole working life in the police, was sympathetic. He had always valued Fabio Volta, and liked the younger man. He sensed that his talent was wasted in his current position. Indeed, he realised that as a man of talent, Volta had been deliberately pushed aside. Storace also saw what Volta saw, though dimly: that the police had lost the fight against organised crime, for the temptations that organised crime commanded were simply too great for the men and women in uniform. The greatest temptation was to cut corners, to get even with one's enemies, by calling in the friends. He had heard about the Perraino case; he knew signora Perraino's reputation, though he had never met her. He had heard of the aunt, Anna Maria Tancredi. He knew that having done this favour for Perraino, Perraino was forever in their debt. He would certainly be promoted. And he would not be the only one.

As it turned out, Storace found a way back to Sicily for Volta. A certain political party with which he had a marked sympathy, and which traded on a law and order platform, and which crusaded against corruption, was looking for someone to work in its research department. Storace had not spent all his life in the police without making a few useful friends. A job was going in the Catania office of the party, a job that Volta, he was sure, would do well. It entailed gathering information about organised crime, and about the way the criminals had infiltrated the police, the Church, and the government.

Over lunch, Storace, hearing Volta's tale of woe, mentioned this possibility.

'The official title is head of research or something like that. Naturally, they don't want the whole thing advertised, and they are looking for someone clandestinely. You would be working, not undercover, but discreetly. On the surface, it's an office job. In fact, it is really a job that involves digging for information. If I recommend you – because they trust me – it will be yours. Needless to say, they are very worried that the wrong person will get the job.'

'The wrong person?'

'A friend, of the friends. Someone in their debt. That would nullify the whole operation. But you, I think, are above suspicion.'

When the offer came, to return to Catania and work in political research, to start in that autumn, he happily threw in his non-career with the police and took it. But there was one last thing the police force could do for him, even though it was not strictly speaking legal. He had long been fascinated, even obsessed by the Vitale case, and the case of the Chemist, and to this interest he had added the case of Carmine del Monaco. He remembered Rosario di Rienzi well, whom he had last seen as a twelve-year-old. That the teenager had left his family and moved to Rome was of interest to him, and he strove to bring about a meeting between the two of them, feeling that Rosario might, wittingly or not, be a way in to cracking the case of Calogero di Rienzi.

But one could not make a direct approach; one had to go in sideways, as it were. One had to act undercover, almost deceptively. Even if it took him his whole life, Volta was determined that one day he would bring Calogero to book. He remembered his smooth assurance when they had interviewed him. That rankled. They had been made fools of by a teenager. One day he would get even. He was young enough to feel the humiliation of it gnawing away at him. Storace, with whom he had discussed this, was able to put the failure down to experience. But Storace was old and wise and used to failure. He still had to learn that lesson.

It was quite easy to find out where Rosario di Rienzi had gone, quite easy to establish, once one had heard of his flight, who had enabled him to get away, and where he was living and where he was going to school. One merely had to trace who the boy's friends and protectors were: the priest, don Giorgio, and the lawyer Petrocchi.

The priest's motivation was not hard to understand. One assumed that he loathed Calogero. Volta remembered meeting him in the hotel carpark at Acitrezza after the wedding. This was not a man who had any sympathy with the elder brother, and who had presumably taken pity on the younger for that very reason. As for the lawyer, he seemed to take a more nuanced position. He had let Calogero into the Confraternity, and at the same time sponsored the flight of Rosario. Did this represent a betting on both horses?

He too was betting on a horse. He was looking at Calogero and thinking he would go far. One thing was certain, as far as he could see: Calogero di Rienzi, now that he had started, would never stop. He might think he could join the respectable legal world, but he was surely too addicted to the drug of power ever to renounce the weapons that he held in his hand. Having known the intoxication of what it was like to be feared, how could he give that up? Yes, he was betting on a horse: he was betting that Calogero would rise to the top, and that he would follow his career and one day, when he was at the top, pull him down. For just as the seeds of his future eminence were now clear, so too, if he could only find them out, would be the seeds of his future destruction.

And so, a year after the murder of Carmine del Monaco, before he was due to return to Catania, and take up his new job, he decided that he would make his move to try and talk to Rosario. His expertise with teenage boys was limited. He was not married and he was an only child; he knew nothing about football, which he naively supposed to be the chief teenage preoccupation; but he thought there was another way into winning the confidence of Rosario di Rienzi, and that was religion. The boy, as far as he could remember, was the archetypal good boy of Italian culture, a young priest in the making, and really all one had to do was lie in wait in the various churches around where he was now living and one was sure to meet him. And there, in the quietness of a Roman church, perhaps, rather differently from a police station, one could perhaps gain the youngster's confidence.

Three years later, in the sunshine of early summer, a young man of eighteen sat on the Spanish Steps in Rome. It was Sunday afternoon and the steps were crowded. Rosario di Rienzi sat on his own, whereas everyone else around him was in some sort of crowd of friends. This was, he knew, from his experience of school, which had ended the previous year, the Roman way, the Italian way. It was the same at the University. Everyone fled from solitude; isolation was bad; everyone sought to be with as many people as they possibly could as much of the time as they could. By contrast, he himself, though he found social relations quite easy, was always conscious of the solitude that he carried around within himself. Even in a crowd like this one, a noisy crowd, he felt alone; he was a Sicilian among Italians, a provincial among Romans, a man with sisters and a brother, but without sisters and a brother; a son without a father; a son without a mother. He was, in so social a setting, an oddity.

The boys and girls he had been at school with had been friendly without becoming fast friends; they had spoken, but every conversation had eventually reached a blank wall. Why was he in Rome? Why was he not in Catania with his family? Why did he speak with such an unmistakeable Sicilian accent? Who were his parents? Who were his family? Where was his home? All these were conversation-stopping questions. How could he begin to answer them when he did not know the answer himself? He was the son of a criminal, that was for sure. His father had been a mass murderer, the infamous Chemist. Of course, because he had not changed his name, they all knew this. The Chemist was now part of the lore of Italian crime. The Chemist had ranged freely over the peninsula, undetected for decades, dealing out death and destruction. The person he had hardly known himself, was now known to all, a recognised figure, a character, a person whose career summed up everything that was wrong with the country.

'It must be hard for you being the son of the Chemist,' was one of the things that Fabio Volta had said to him, a remark that had at once opened a channel of communication. For it was true. It was a nightmare being the son of that man, the murderer; the guilt he felt was terrible. That Fabio Volta should realise this was the case established an understanding between them.

His school, a private school run by the Christian Brothers, was one of the best in Rome, and filled with the children of the rich. He knew they knew he was the Chemist's son, and this had at first worried him a great deal. It was possible, for example, that his father had been responsible for the deaths of people they had known, for it was not inconceivable that among the boys and girls of his class were some related to the various government officials who had been blown up by the Chemist; or related to the various people in railway stations who had fallen victim to his bombs. If they were to shun him, or to hate him, or want to be revenged on him, that would not surprise him in the least. That was what one would expect. A punch in the kidneys, the disappearance of one's books, the turning away in the corridor. But in fact that was not quite what happened.

What happened was somewhat harder to deal with. He realised that amidst these members of the Roman bourgeoisie, he was an object of some fascination. He was touched with the faint glamour of a life so different they could hardly picture it. He was child of the slums, for a start, the slums of Catania. Most of his classmates had been to Sicily on holiday. Many of them had stayed in luxury hotels in Taormina with views of Mount Etna, or else wandered the spectacular beach and townscape of Cefalù; he had never been to either place, only seen pictures. They knew nothing of the Sicily he knew, and their imaginations led them wildly astray, when they tried to picture the Purgatory quarter of Catania, with what they imagined to be its narrow fetid streets, with washing extended from one side to the other, its decaying walls, and its criminals hanging about at every street corner. It wasn't quite like that, though, but the way it really was, he could not explain. Everyone, it seemed to him, was trapped in their own version of normality, without having any real insight into the normality of others. Each spoke a language that was untranslatable.

His classmates all had brothers and sisters and fathers and mothers; and the family he lived with was just that, a family. They were very pleasant people, and lived in a nineteenth century block on the Via Merulana, very close to the Lateran Basilica. From there he walked to school quite easily. The father was a functionary at the ministry of the Interior on the Viminal hill; the mother was a doctor; they were known to the lawyer Petrocchi and approved of by don Giorgio; they were prosperous people and very good Catholics. There was a boy at University, older than himself, and a girl a year or so younger; as he watched them interact, he was surprised in so many ways; it was like watching animals in a zoo. One wondered at how different they were from oneself, while at the same time seeing faint resemblances. His own family, he now saw, had been outwardly human, but inwardly quite different. Signor Carducci never hit his son. Signora Carducci was solicitous towards her children and towards himself, and seemed to mean it; indeed, she did mean it, and after a time he began to understand that she was what she seemed, a very kind and concerned mother to the children and foster mother to himself. Moreover, his personal space was entirely respected. No one ever went through his school bag, or rummaged through his clothes as Calogero had always done. No one hit him, or ignored the fact that he was being hit. When he was in bed, no one ever tried to get into bed with him and hold him in a tight suffocating embrace. There was privacy: it was as if every human being was an inviolable sanctuary, never to be trampled upon, a sacred space never to be profaned.

This was one of the things that he had discussed with Fabio Volta, after their first few meetings that had taken place in the Lateran Basilica. Was it possible, he wanted to know, that personal relations could be conducted without the threat of violence? Could one be with other people on terms where one would not hit the other when disagreement arose? Was it possible to have two people in some sort of relationship where it was not a case of one was the one who was hit, and the other the one who did the hitting?

Fabio Volta was intrigued to learn that the Chemist had regularly beaten his eldest son, with some ferocity too, until Calogero had reached the age of fourteen when he had been treated like an adult. And that Calogero had regularly beaten Rosario and Turiddu, and any child who had got in his way. However, the Chemist and Calogero had never hit women, presumably because they did not need to. At least that was Rosario's way of looking at it. The women were utterly subservient to them. It was children who bore the brunt of the violence at home. Then there were the cases of the various murders: Vitale, Carmine del Monaco, and the savage beating of the policemen Fabrizio Perraino. Power, in the end, came down to the use of the fist, and relations were based on power. Were other ways of relating possible?

Fabio had considered this, and they had discussed this at length. Seeing everything in religious terms, Rosario maintained that the opposite of power was love, which was the renunciation of power. Outside the Lateran Basilica stood the statues of Saint Francis and his companions, who had walked to Rome from Umbria, dressed as beggars, barefoot, to see the Pope. That represented the way of renunciation, rather than the way of seizing everything for oneself by force. Fabio Volta, being a man of law enforcement, saw the opposite of power as law: law that was to be administered without fear or favour, with complete neutrality. It seemed

163

to Rosario that neutrality was never going to command human loyalty or satisfy the human desire for sympathy and love.

This desire, for sympathy and love, he felt very strongly. If his father had not been a true father to him, which was hard to contradict, the example of signora Carducci drove home to him the failure of his own mother to be a true mother. She had not protected him from Calogero; she had known, and turned away from the knowledge of what she had known. She had in fact shut herself off from all knowledge that was inconvenient or challenging. As a result, she had lived in peace but the peace she lived in was the terrible peace of suspended animation. She had killed maternal feeling. The price for her life was a living death. He felt sorry for her, but at the same time he loathed the very thought of her. He had needed a mother, and she had failed him. He had needed someone to protect him, and he had also needed someone to love him, and she had failed on both counts. The painfulness of this failure, brought home to him by the contrasting example of signora Carducci, meant that he never wanted to see his mother again. To see her again would be to feel the pain of loss; for though he now thought he had never known maternal love, he still felt what could have been his as a loss almost too hard to bear.

He had explained all this to Fabio, who was good listener. Fabio, who like all Italians, was close to his mother, was shocked. It seemed to him that Rosario was one of that small minority of boys whose mother had died; but this was worse. She was still alive, but unreachable. He pointed out that one day, God willing, Rosario would find someone to replace his mother, namely a wife. But Rosario heard this in silence, knowing that a wife was as unreachable as a mother for him.

For there were other loves too that he had to renounce, for there were other comforts that he felt which would only make his misery worse. He had to be detached from humanity, because he had already seen too much of humanity at its worst. The daughter of the house, Maria Carducci, had gone to the same school as he did, and they had walked back from school at various times and she had taken his hand, which he felt was delightful; later on, on one occasion when they were both alone, she had made an attempt to kiss him, but he had rebuffed her. It would not be wise, he realised, to fall in love with his host family's only daughter, or to let her fall in love with him. It would not be wise to fall in love at all. To fall in love with someone would be to drag them into the ugly vortex in which he lived; it would be to connect them to the Chemist and his world, Calogero and his world. One could not inflict that on anyone. As for getting married and having children, having a family in a world where the concept of family had been so perverted, that was an unspeakable prospect.

On Saturday and Sunday afternoons he would often go for a walk around the quarter in which he now lived; he would visit the Villa Celimontana, the most lovely of all Roman parks, and he would visit the grandiose basilica of the Lateran, and the basilica of Holy Cross. Often, until he had to go back to Catania, Fabio Volta would join him for these walks, and it was during these walks that they became fast friends. There was something astonishing about Rome. He was familiar with the Roman ruins in Catania, the amphitheatre in Terpsichore Square, the theatre that was built into the houses in the Via Vittorio Emanuele, and also the places associated with Saint Agatha. But at the Lateran you could see the bronze doors of the Senate House, which would have been familiar to Julius Caesar; at Holy Cross you could sense the presence of the Empress Helen and see the relics of the Passion of the Lord. It wasn't the antiquity of it all that struck him, but its nearness. This was not a world that was far away, but one that one could almost reach out and touch. But his favourite church was undoubtedly Four Crowned Saints, where he would go to Mass every day very early in the morning, accompanied by one, two or three, sometimes all four of the Carduccis. There the cloistered nuns sang in a church that had not changed in a thousand years. In the apse, rendered in fresco, the saints of the Church rejoiced, each brandishing the instrument of their martyrdom. And in that Church, before the altar, he made the daily vow that he would never marry, but would remain a virgin forever, and dedicate his life to God.

His mother had perhaps once loved his father; but if she had never married him, her life would have been happier, he felt. As for Calogero and his wife, as he sat on the Spanish Steps, alone on the crowd, he thought of his sister-in-law Stefania. She was Calogero's age, four years his senior, and they had barely spoken a word to each other. That age gap was considerable. He had been a child when she had married Calogero. Had she loved him? Why had she married him? Who could know the answer? But she would certainly regret marrying him one day, he was sure.

The person he was now waiting for was in fact Stefania. She had written to him, asking for this meeting. His immediate reaction was to refuse her request, but he had consulted Fabio Volta and Fabio had persuaded him to meet her. In fact, he was glad to do so, in a way, and needed little persuasion. He had for the last three summers visited Catania, but he had not approached any member of his family or even entered the Purgatory quarter, though he very much would have liked to visit the Church of the Holy Souls in Purgatory. He had worked as an intern in the office of the lawyer Petrocchi, and lived in the house of a priest in Acireale, which had been arranged by don Giorgio. The lawyer's office had provided interesting work, and in the evenings, he had helped the priest in Acireale run the oratorio, the youth club that kept the local children busy all summer. It had been perfectly pleasant, though even on the Via Etnea one could sense the darkness of the Purgatory quarter only a few hundred metres away.

He wondered why Stefania wanted to see him. It could hardly be curiosity, or anything personal, given that they barely knew each other. Was she coming as an envoy of his brother Calogero? In which case, it was a slightly unusual choice. His mother might have come instead, or more naturally his sisters. But perhaps Caloriu had the penetration to see that he would have rejected any meeting with his mother out of hand, and been most unwilling to meet either of his sisters too, given that they had made no attempt to contact him for the last three years. His sisters could have done so; they would only have had to ask don Giorgio, or given him a letter to hand on to him. But they had been silent. He had deserted the family, and they treated him as a guilty thing. And if Caloriu had sent Stefania, what could Caloriu possibly want from him? This was intriguing, and this was the real reason he had decided, when her letter had come, forwarded from don Giorgio, that he would meet her. She would perhaps want to find out about him; but he in his turn would try to find out about Calogero. They would not use him, but he would use her. During the last two summers he had seen a great deal of Fabio Volta, as well as don Giorgio. It was during these two summers that Fabio Volta had effectively turned him; and he had done so because he wanted to be turned.

And so she came, as he sat there on the Steps in the sun, and she was close to him before he even noticed her. In fact he would have had difficulty recognising her, so effectively had he blocked her and everything to do with his brother from his memory. Besides which, in the three years he had not seen her, she had changed. She was less of a girl, more of a woman. Her figure had filled out, and she was smartly and expensively dressed. She was everything one would expect a rich bourgeoise to be: the shoes, the bag, the dress, the dark glasses, the carefully done natural looking blonde hair. Quite a beautiful woman, he thought. And then he wondered if she had taken all this trouble just for him? Or was this who she now was, the rich wife of a rich man? Someone who had risen in the world, and yet someone who had the skill to appear as if the position they now occupied was one they had been born into.

While he had had difficulty recognising her, she knew him immediately, and came and sat down on the Steps next to him.

'Hi,' said Stefania, with a smile.

'Hi,' he replied more guardedly.

'My husband, your brother, does not know I am here,' she said. 'I came to see you because I wanted to see you. I mean, Calogero knows that I am in Rome. I have come for the shopping and to see the sights. He knows that. But he does not know that I am seeing you. I asked don Giorgio about you, and, anyway, I am very glad that you have agreed to see me. You look well. Rome agrees with you. It is so lovely here. It is so carefree. Catania is beautiful, but Purgatory is not quite the sort of place where one can relax, though it has changed a great deal of late, as I am sure you will want to know.'

'Why should I want to know?' he asked, feeling that his tone was ruder than it ought to be.

'Curiosity,' she said. 'You left so suddenly. You must want to know how it has all got on without you.'

'If you knew why I had left, you would know that the opposite was true. That I have absolutely no desire to see or hear of the place again.'

'I know why you left, at least in part,' she said. 'I am married to your brother, and I understand him better than most people, I think. But you agreed to see me, and so I think that perhaps you do want to know, almost in spite of yourself. If only to know that your decision to leave was the right thing to do.'

'It was the only thing to do,' he said.

'Yes, I suppose it was,' she said. 'But sometimes the passage of time makes you re-evaluate things. I married Calogero because it was the only thing to do. That was five years ago, but it seems like a lifetime. If I were to re-evaluate that decision, I would marry him again, but not for the same reasons. I have learned a lot in the last five years.'

'Why did you marry him?'

'Silly reasons,' said Stefania. 'He wanted to marry me. That was the main reason. Because in Purgatory every girl who invests her time in a boy wants to bring that investment to maturity at the altar. And Calogero has some charm, you know. He uses it when he wants to. And he is physically attractive, or at least he was. He has put on a lot of weight recently, and refuses to diet. But none of the reasons I had for marrying him were good reasons.'

'And now?'

'And now being married to Calogero means a huge opportunity for me. An undreamed of opportunity. I will explain. But we cannot sit here all day. I have booked a place for lunch. Let us go there.'

They walked the length of the Via della Croce and crossed the Corso until they came to a large modern restaurant near the tomb of Augustus.

'I have a credit card,' she said. 'And I have a mobile phone. Calogero has neither still. Well, he has a card, but he only uses it rarely. Everything is usually in cash, and no one can trace where he has been or what he has spent. He has a naturally suspicious mind. He assumes they are watching him and tracking him every step of the way.'

'Who are they?'

'The anonymous they. The they that changes every moment. The government, the police, the Carabinieri, the Finance police; the Church, the State; the people who are not us. The people one must never trust. The people who are behind the scenes and who manipulate everything. The people who killed your father. The people Calogero fears.'

'My father killed himself.'

'Yes, he did. I know that. But Calogero, who must know that too, thinks that it was all an elaborate conspiracy. The anonymous they went around blowing people up for years and years, getting rid of the people they did not like, creating tensions for their own advantages, and then they framed an innocent man and blamed him for everything that had happened. An elaborate theory that requires a little too much elaboration in my opinion. My late father-in-law did what they said he did, though there are still questions. Who was he working for? Another anonymous they. Whose purpose was served by all these crimes? Some of them were just senseless. The bombs in railways stations, for example.'

'We will never understand it fully,' said Rosario. 'And Calogero fears them, you say? Is he really frightened of anyone?'

'He is terrified,' she said. 'Not in the normal sense, of course. But he sees the world as a deeply hostile environment. A savage place, where only savages, such as himself, prosper. And where prosperity never lasts for long. But you understand that surely? That's why he was so cruel to you. He fears you.'

They ordered their food.

'That waiter does not like Sicilians,' she continued. 'You can see it in his face when he heard our voices. He feels that we should not be here, that we are interlopers, invaders. We should go back to where we came from. They think we are Arabs.'

'That's the people from Palermo. We are Greeks,' said Rosario with a smile, the first he had allowed himself. 'The name Calogero is Greek, didn't you know. It means 'fair old age' or something like that. Kalos means beautiful in ancient Greek and good in modern Greek. Ironic, I think you will agree.'

'He was handsome in certain lights, when he was young, when he was a teenager, but neither beautiful nor good, I agree. With you they chose the right name. The man of the Rosary, the man of the Blessed Virgin Mary. They got that right. My name is Greek too, and means crown, doesn't it? But to get back to my husband and your brother, he has changed a great deal since you left.'

'In what way?' he asked, trying not to sound interested.

'He has become rich and important. More than that: he has become accepted.'

'That is awful.'

The waiter came with the first courses.

'It was just after the rescue of the Spanish Madonna,' she said. 'That was when his fortunes changed, well, our fortunes changed. That's when everything moved up a gear. That was when the lawyer Petrocchi admitted him to the Confraternity of the Holy Souls in Purgatory. Don Giorgio was not pleased at all, but Petrocchi insisted. I am not sure why. Shortly after that, Calogero borrowed an immense sum of money from the bank – and used it to buy up as many empty apartments and buildings in Purgatory as he could. At the same time, he got rid of many of the old tenants who were, in his view, pulling down the reputation of the quarter. He spent a fortune on doing up the places he bought or which he newly liberated –'

'You mean, he got rid of the prostitutes?' asked Rosario. 'How very cruel of him. Poor women. They were just chucked out into the street?'

'Yes.'

Rosario was thoughtful. He wondered if that included Romanian Anna. Was she now completely destitute? He knew her, because her son Traiano had been another of the altar servers at the Church of the Holy Souls in Purgatory. Don Giorgio had always been very kind to the child Traiano. As for Anna, he, Rosario, knew her by sight, and he knew that Calogero had lost his virginity with her at the age of thirteen. It had been a very frequently boasted of fact. Had he now driven her out? He could hardly ask.

'Yes. He got rid of them,' his sister-in-law was saying. 'But only to replace them with other higher-class ones, less noticeable ones. Now, you would not recognise the place. It is full of tourists, there are several new bars and restaurants. It is quite transformed in three years, many of the flats he bought are now rented out to short stay tourists but his aim is to get in long term tenants and to make the place fashionable. He is succeeding. You see, your brother was always clever.'

'And he never had any compunction about going around the law, or beyond the law, when he needed to,' said Rosario. 'I can't criticise the lawyer Petrocchi who paid for my school fees and now pays for me to go to university. I have worked in his office for three summers, so if I were to criticise him it would be hypocrisy on my part. But I know what my brother has got up to. People talk. The lawyer Rossi, do you know him? Yes, of course you do. He is a terrible gossip. Everyone knows that properties in the decayed heart of Catania are cheap to buy because they have sitting tenants and the law makes it almost impossible to get rid of such tenants, and the rents are often fixed at absurdly low levels. Which is why such places are never maintained – a vicious circle. Well, Calogero uniquely seems to be able to dislodge sitting tenants. How does he do that?'

'You know how he does that,' she said. 'Once he did it himself. Now he wears a suit and Turiddu does it for him.'

'He has franchised out the threats. And does Turiddu still steal wallets and mug strangers in the quarter?'

'No,' she said. 'That is bad for property prices. The place is completely safe these days. No street crime at all, by order of Calogero. If anyone tried anything, Turiddu is sent to sort them out. No drug trading, except very discretely in one of the bars. That attracts a lot of people, young people. Turiddu controls all that. That is his reward.'

'Everything unsavoury he leaves to Turiddu,' said Rosario bitterly. 'Apart from the stuff that the lawyer Rossi does for him.'

'You know the lawyer Rossi?'

'I have spent three summers working in the office with him. I know he does work for Calogero. I asked him to let me see my father's will.'

'And?'

'He refused, of course. First he said he didn't have anything to do with it. Then he admitted that he may have done. Then he said he didn't have a copy. Then he said he had had a copy, but he didn't think he could find it. That went on for weeks. At the end, I realised I didn't need to see the will at all. My suspicions were confirmed. If the will were completely correct, he would have shown it to me. His guilty reaction was a sign of, well, guilt.'

'Yes,' she said. 'Rossi was just an instrument. It was Calogero who made him do it. He must have threatened to break his neck. Or else to take his business elsewhere. Rossi has done well out of Calogero. And Calogero had done well out of Rossi. Everyone like Calogero needs a tame lawyer. Icing on the cake. Underneath the cake may not be great, but as long as the icing is correct it looks like a proper cake. But he cheated you, he cheated his sisters, he cheated his own mother.'

'I know he did, but I do not care. Petrocchi mentioned it to me, for he had his suspicions, and said he could arrange for Caloriu to compensate me. I told him I was not interested. Perhaps Petrocchi who has been supporting me has received compensation from Caloriu. That would be his business. But I want nothing to do with Calogero's money. It all started with the fees my father was paid for murdering innocent people. It's tainted.'

'Money has no smell,' said Stefania. 'All great fortunes started off in questionable ways. All the great ones of the earth were once robber barons. There is hardly anyone who can say that their money was got in purely good ways, through sheer hard work. Money comes to you through luck, through taking advantage of other people and the opportunities that you are offered. Calogero has taken lots of opportunities, lots of short cuts.'

'Don't defend him,' said Rosario. 'Killing Vitale was more than just a short cut.'

'You know about that, do you?'

'I do know about it. Thank you for reminding me of my guilt. I was his alibi. You were his alibi. We are both complicit. And then there is the case of Carmine del Monaco. I was not there for that, I was hundreds of miles away, but I know he was involved. After all, he stole the Spanish Madonna and planted it in the pizzeria to make it look as though Carmine del Monaco had done so.'

'You are sure?'

'That he stole the Spanish Madonna? Positive. He used my key. And the del Monaco murder – he was involved in that. It may have been someone else who stabbed the man, but he arranged it.'

'That night he was triumphant,' she said, 'I remember.'

'And in his triumph you share,' Rosario could not resist adding.

She looked at him.

'Can you blame me?' she said. 'When you see a ladder, don't you want to climb up it? There is some news about Turiddu, had you heard?'

He shook his head.

'He has got a girlfriend. He has had her for some time. She is the Romanian woman called Anna, double his age. She is about thirty-three, and she has a son not that much younger now than Turiddu. He has been living with her for the last three years. Calogero gave them a nice flat.'

'I remember Anna the Romanian. She used to come to church. Her son was an altar server. So, Calogero has been kind to them. Or rather kind to Turiddu. In return for what? He gives nothing away for free.'

'I don't know,' she admitted. 'Anyway, that child Turiddu -though he is the same age as you – has been living with this Anna for the last three years. Anna now works in one of the bars as manager. She came here, well, she worked as a whore when she started, but now, thanks to Turiddu and Calogero, she's respectable. Like the whole of Purgatory. Moving up in the world. I assumed that Turiddu was living with her because he didn't want to live at home with his parents. I thought she was more of a mother figure. In fact, it seems that the flat had two bedrooms, and Turiddu was sharing with the little boy, who is called Traiano, and who is about twelve or thirteen. But it seems he must have slipped into Anna's bed, because she is pregnant and says it is his. The whole thing is very strange... He wanted to impregnate her to increase his status; she wanted to have his child to secure her status. It is a pregnancy of convenience. And Calogero is furious.'

'Why would he be?' asked Rosario, though he could guess. But it was her reasoning that he wanted to hear.

'You don't know how his mind works. We have two daughters – I notice you have not asked me about your nieces, but never mind, in fact you have never ever seen Natalia, have you – and Calogero wants a son. He badly wants a son. To continue the family name, to prove to the world he can father a son, to show his credentials as a man of a great family. And now Turiddu has done the unforgiveable thing, he has beaten his master to it.'

'It may not be a son,' Rosario pointed out.

'They had an ultrasound that shows that it is, and they have been showing everyone who is interested, and quite a few who are not. It provoked Calogero. When we had the ultrasound to look at Natalia in the womb and saw she was a girl he was bitterly disappointed, for the second time. He does not like ultrasounds. They depress him. In fact, my guess was that the whole thing was designed to provoke Calogero.'

'You mean Turi made Anna pregnant to annoy my brother? An odd motive.'

'But what do you know about the history between those two?' she asked levelly.

Rosario was silent. He remembered. He had the image of his brother sharing a bed with Turiddu years ago, when Turiddu was very young (something he had done with himself too) and Caloriu getting out of bed, in a hurry, in his underwear.

'Who understands the history between those two?' he asked. 'Not me. And I don't want to know.'

'Anyway, Calogero went to see Turiddu and there was huge fight.'

'A physical fight?'

'Indeed yes. Is there ever any other type in our part of the world? Turiddu ended up badly hurt. And words were exchanged. I don't know who said what to whom, but insults were exchanged. The boy Traiano was traumatised. These were lots of screams from Anna the mother. Then Calogero left, leaving an ultimatum. That Anna was to have an abortion, or else.'

'Or else what?'

'I think it was a threat to either kill the child, or be killed himself,' she said.

'Is this what you came here to tell me?' asked Rosario. 'That Calogero is going to kill Turiddu? It's hardly unexpected. There is no honour among thieves, and Turiddu has served his purpose.'

'You don't seem sorry,' she said.

'I loathe Turiddu,' he said. 'You must realise that. It is interesting to note that you must do as well.'

'Yes,' she said. 'I do.' She paused. 'You just have to sit back, and Calogero will do everything you have always wanted to do to Turiddu yourself. And I too am in a similar position.'

'You attribute to me the basest motives, the motive for revenge.'

'It's what we all want,' she said crisply.

There was silence between them; the plates were cleared, and the main courses arrived.

'My gnocchi were not particularly good,' said Stefania.

'Why haven't you given him a son?' asked Rosario. 'If that is what he wants so badly.'

She smiled.

'My husband, your brother, is not as attentive to me as he might be. It is not that I keep him waiting. Or that I think that when he gets rid of Turiddu, then it may well be time for me to have a son. That until then, he keeps on being disappointed. He is not frustrated, I am. Your brother, well, it is hard to say: he is good at threatening people, at beating them

179

up, but the tender arts of love are difficult for him. Making himself agreeable is hard for him. That intimidates him. You have just finished the first year at University, haven't you?'

'Yes.'

'When Turiddu is dead, and I do not see him as surviving much longer, and when all the criminal past is behind him, Calogero will need you. You are clean, and you are his brother. You will be beyond reproach. You will sanitise everything, for Calogero, for me, for my children.'

He could see her point in all its clarity.

'There is only one thing you have not thought of,' he said. 'Calogero may be planning to kill Turiddu. But Turiddu may act first. Have you thought of that?'

She shrugged.

'Then I inherit everything.'

'No. Then he inherits everything.' There was silence between them. 'Can either you or I compete with them? We don't have the muscle power. And does it matter in the end, who is rich and who is not, as long as we have enough to live on?'

'Do you want to spend your life dependant on others?' she asked. 'Do you want to be a second class citizen for the rest of your life?'

He didn't answer the question.

'Caloriu will move slowly. He is a strategic thinker. You watch.'

'When are you coming back?'

'In July,' he replied. 'The lawyer Petrocchi expects me.'

'So will I,' she said.

Chapter Eight

Traiano had been about three years old, and far too young to remember, when he had witnessed his father almost beat his mother to death. Since that unhappy time, he and his mother had had better experiences, in coming to Sicily, in living in Purgatory, a place which was far nicer in every way, in the boy's mind, than the city of Iasi they had left behind, a place he associated with tales of bad food, boiling summers and freezing winters. Here in Catania, it was never too hot, and never too cold, and the food was excellent. Here in Catania, so that his mother could work, he went to school every day. He had not forgotten his native language, for his mother had never given up trying to get him to remember it. But Catania had become his home. It had been his home so long, now that he was almost twelve years old, that he felt he had little connection to Romania, apart from his name.

He loved his mother, and he liked all the women of the quarter, all of whom made a huge fuss over him, exclaiming whenever they saw him that he was the most beautiful child they had ever seen; but even though he knew that was why his mother had left his father and taken him away, he missed his father. He missed the idea of his father's extended family, he missed the thought of his grandparents, his uncles and his aunts. Of course, his father was a bad-tempered man, he had been told that, but he was still his father. In his experience, all men were bad tempered to some extent.

His mother had assured him that his father was still her husband, and that he would never be replaced. In fact his mother had made it clear to the boy what she believed, which was what everyone ought to believe: that once married in the sight of God, nothing on earth could ever dissolve that bond.

Then Turiddu had entered their lives. Turiddu was only five and half years his senior, which in one sense was not much, but in another sense was an infinite distance in years. When they lived in the single room, Turiddu had slept with his mother on her side of the partition. He did not know what they were doing there, but his real question was why did Turiddu have to sleep in their house at all? Didn't he have a house of his own to go to? It struck him that they would all be happier without Turiddu. But his mother, who sensed he felt this, told him that this was not the way to think. Turiddu was very kind to them.

And so it proved, for thanks to Turiddu, they all moved to the new big flat, where there were two bedrooms. His had two beds in it and sometimes Turiddu would be asleep in the other bed when he woke in the morning. It seemed that Turiddu was often busy at nights and would come in very late without waking him. His mother worked in the bar, and Turiddu was often in the bar, and they both finished work very late. Sometimes they would take it in turns to look after him. He loved the evenings at home with his mother, when they would watch television together. The evenings at home alone with Turiddu were less enjoyable. Turiddu brought into the house an air of disorder with him. He sprawled on the sofa and looked cross, and Traiano felt he had to be very quiet in front of him. He made him watch the programmes he wanted to watch, whereas his mother let him choose. He often fell asleep on the sofa and snored. He never made much effort to speak to him. Except on one topic. He often asked Traiano about Calogero.

Traiano had known Calogero since their arrival in Catania. That is to say, he had known Calogero ever since he had begun to remember things. When he had been six, he had seen Calogero standing in the square outside the Church of the Holy Souls in Purgatory, boys much bigger than himself surrounding him, and he remembered the thrill he had felt when Calogero had first noticed him, first deigned to speak to him. For there was no doubt that Calogero was the idol of the quarter's youth. He had swelled with pleasure when Calogero had asked him what his name was, who his mother was, where he lived, and given him a euro. In those days,

Calogero had often dressed in a tracksuit and sported a gold chain around his neck. Later, this had changed to a pair of Armani jeans and an expensive shirt, and he had hidden the chain. More recently, Calogero had taken to wearing a suit and highly polished shoes, which were, they said, all bought for him by his wife Stefania, who flew to Milan for the purpose of buying her own clothes and her husband's too. Calogero was smart and cool in Traiano's eyes, in every respect, and always generous. As he had got older, Calogero had paid him more attention. He had often asked him to take verbal messages to people in the quarter - 'Go and find so and so, tell him I will be coming to see him in twenty minutes'- using a child rather than a mobile phone, and Traiano loved this, because it showed that he was trusted and liked, and often these requests would be accompanied by Calogero stuffing a five, ten or even twenty euro note into his pocket before he ran off to do his will.

Of course, Turiddu knew this, and Traiano was guarded in what he said about Calogero. His mother had told him that they depended on Calogero's kindness for the house they lived in. This was confusing: sometimes their principal benefactor was Turiddu, sometimes Calogero. And yet not so confusing really, because it was clear to him that Calogero counted for far more than Turiddu; if one had to choose who to offend, it had to be Turiddu, not Calogero. Never Calogero.

Sometimes Turiddu's questions were very strange. He would ask whether he had ever been alone with Calogero. He would ask whether Calogero would ever come up to the flat when his mother was out. He would ask whether he himself had ever been in Calogero's house. The answer to all this was no, of course. He only ever saw Calogero in the square or in the street. But Turiddu persisted in these questions.

Traiano was not stupid, and he knew what Turiddu was fishing for. Like most eleven-year olds, he knew all about that sort of thing, and had been warned by his mother to beware of strange men. But at the same time his mother told him that he need not worry about Uncle Calogero, and whatever Uncle Calogero asked him to do, he should do.

Once he heard his mother and Turiddu shouting at each other.

'You wouldn't prostitute yourself any more,' he heard him say. 'But you would use your son.'

He didn't understand this at all. But he noticed how upset his mother was for days afterwards, and he did his best to comfort her. That Turiddu upset his mother made him dislike Turiddu even more than he did already. Then came the news that his mother was to have a baby, and the baby's father was Turiddu.

Anna's pregnancy was something of a scandal in Purgatory. Everyone knew (even her son, even though she had tried her best to shield him from the knowledge) that she had been a prostitute, but had been rescued from the profession by Turiddu, and installed as manager of one of the new bars which Calogero owned. No one in the quarter was prepared to hold this against her; after all, we all have our pasts, and we all try to forget them, and why should others remember what we ourselves have chosen to forget? Besides, there was no great shame in her former calling. Many were the prostitutes who had lived in the quarter and who had been kindly women respected by all. Anna had fled Romania and an abusive husband and had had to provide for her child. So, the women did not blame her for what she had done; indeed they admired the way she had risen from the lowest profession and made something of herself. As for the men of the quarter, some of whom had used her services, they too respected and liked her: she was good-looking, polite and respectful, and her son was a credit to her. She ran the bar well, and though it was a place where all sorts of assignations were made, nevertheless it had a decent air about it.

As for her relationship with Turiddu, here there was much discussion. Turiddu had taken up with Anna at the age of fifteen, but it was held by almost all who cared to discuss these things, that the relationship never went further than friendship. He would share a bed with her and no more. This was widely assumed. Some knew, and whispered, that Turiddu had exotic tastes, and that one of the new girls working in the quarter would see him from time to time and, for a considerable fee, provide him with what he liked, namely to be tied up, whipped and defecated upon. This news was passed on by word of mouth with puzzled interest. Some people liked that sort of thing. For the girls who specialised in it, it was a good line of work to have, as their clients tended to be very quiet and respectable people, and included many lawyers and policemen. And if this were generally known in the quarter, that Turiddu frequented a sado-masochistic prostitute (a very nice girl, often to be seen in the market outside the Church of the Holy Souls in Purgatory in the morning), if they all knew, one could be sure that Calogero knew, and used this knowledge or was storing it for future use.

Thus it came as a shock when it was known that Anna was pregnant and Turiddu was the father. It was Turiddu who let this be known. Anna perhaps might have liked less publicity, it was thought. But when Anna was approached, and women liked to talk, the truth emerged. Turiddu and she did share a bed, and generally Turiddu would suck on her nipples and fall asleep with his head against her breasts, which, everyone agreed, were warm, ample, shapely and ideal for that purpose. Very occasionally, he would get an erection and enter her, but this was so rare that she did not think it worthwhile taking precautions, and this was the result. But of course she wasn't sorry; Turiddu was not a good man, but it was important to keep him happy, and to make him feel important, as he was the one who paid for everything. He was making a great deal of money as the sole supplier of cocaine in the quarter, a commodity that foreign visitors and a few locals flocked to buy. Of course, said Anna, one knew about the girl who tied him up and whipped him and other things, but it was important for Turiddu, like all men, to prove to the world that he was normal. Of course he wasn't; no man was normal; but they all liked to think they were. That was one of the things you noticed when you worked with men.

The women who heard this nodded. It accorded with their experience too.

Men. They ran the world. But they did it so badly, because they could barely run themselves.

'But what about your husband in Romania?' asked one of the women.

They all knew that story.

'I have not heard very much from him for six years, nearly,' said Anna. 'I don't expect to hear from him again.'

The same question had been put to her by don Giorgio. Anna was devoted to don Giorgio, who had always been kind to her, ever since she had arrived in Purgatory, and it had been to him that she had first confided the news of her pregnancy. Traiano was one of his altar servers, and Anna had always gone to the early Mass at the Church of the Holy Souls in Purgatory on Sunday mornings. Don Giorgio knew that she was a good Catholic woman, who had striven to bring her son up well, and who had been forced by circumstances to earn her living as best she could. He had often urged her to give up prostitution; but then rather regretted it when she had told him that she had, only to take up with Turiddu and Calogero and work in the new bar, which was front for drug-selling and prostitution. Not that she was involved in either, making coffee as she did, and pouring out the Campari. He supposed that this was not sinful it itself,

187

even though sins were going on all around the innocent activity of bar keeping. But it was certainly not good; and it was certainly not good to associate with Turiddu and Calogero. But what could you do? To live in Purgatory was to be entangled in the webs that Calogero wove.

He asked the question about the husband because he knew the husband had been very violent; if he should somehow hear about this, was there not the possibility of a very angry man from Iasi turning up in Purgatory intent on avenging his honour? He might take it out on Turiddu, but he might take it out on her.

Calogero found out about the pregnancy because Traiano told him. This happened in the Church of the Holy Souls in Purgatory, after Mass one Sunday. Calogero, having joined the Confraternity, now went to Mass; this rather annoyed don Giorgio, who once more felt the contradictions of his calling: he was meant to insist people went to Mass; but at the same time he didn't like seeing Calogero there.

'My mother is having a baby,' said Traiano, with a sense that Calogero should know about this, and that he would be rewarded for letting him know this as soon as possible.

'Holy Mary,' said Calogero. He was looking at the Spanish Madonna as he said this. Then he turned to the child: 'What would your father say?'

'I don't know,' said Traiano. 'We do not hear from him, and we do not know where he is. And he does not know where we are.'

'Jesus,' said Calogero, now looking at the crucifix over the high altar. 'Someone should tell him, don't you think?' he remarked to the boy.

It would, thought Calogero, be a neat solution: an enraged Romanian entering the quarter breathing threats, a man with a reputation for violence, and at the end of it, little Turiddu beaten to death. What could be simpler?

Finding out where the man was, he was sure, would be quite simple. He knew the name, the same as his son, and he knew his date of birth from questioning Traiano, and he supposed he had been born in Iasi, and he supposed that he had a criminal record. One of the policemen who frequented the quarter, and who was always polite to Calogero, was only too eager to help with the research. It turned out that there was a man of that name, born on that date, in Iasi, with a criminal record, recorded as married to one Anna, with one son – but, disappointingly, he was in prison in Bucharest, serving ten years for grievous bodily harm, with several years left to run. He sounded like a truly worthless fellow.

That avenue, then, was closed. But the thought of Turiddu being punished for his temerity in getting Anna pregnant, once it had entered Calogero's head, was hard to dislodge. How dare he? Yet he knew his anger and his disdain were not quite rational. After all, hadn't he himself introduced Turiddu to Anna, taken him up to her that Sunday afternoon, taken the child Traiano away, while Turiddu lost his virginity? He himself had slept with Anna as a teenager, and then passed her on – so why was he so annoyed now? Perhaps it was because it offended him that Anna should somehow prefer, if that is what it signified, Turiddu to him. She had not wanted to have his child, but he had not wanted to give her one; but that was not the point. The point was he was jealous and furious about two people who he controlled doing something without his permission. And, as a teenager, he had mounted Anna, then given her to Turiddu; but she was his property, not Turiddu's.

For all these reasons, Calogero decided that he would communicate his displeasure in person, and leave them with no doubt about his anger. He had keys to all the flats he owned, and thus he could enter Anna's house without knocking, unannounced. He did so when the whole family were around the table in the kitchen having lunch. It was a Sunday, and as he opened the door, he sensed an atmosphere of jocularity, along with the smell of food. He came and stood in the kitchen doorway, and gradually suddenly the conversation died. Traiano alone looked up, delighted to see him. Anna was horrified. She understood. Turiddu was merely sullen.

'Traiano,' said Anna, 'Go to your bedroom. This is adult business.'

He looked at his mother in confusion.

'No, no, no,' said Calogero. 'Let him stay. He may learn something.'

Turiddu was silent.

'You think you have been very clever, don't you?' said Calogero. 'What is it that you are trying to prove?'

'I am not trying to prove anything,' said Turiddu. 'I don't need to. We know it is a boy. They told us at the hospital. I am going to have son before you ever do.'

'You have done this to make me look bad,' said Calogero sadly. 'Or have you done it so that I take notice of you? Have you done it because you want to provoke me? Do you feel neglected?'

Turiddu muttered some Sicilian words the others could not understand. But Calogero understood.

'You have been well rewarded,' he said. 'I would like to strip you naked and beat you with my belt until you bled, and then piss on you. I'd like to do to you what I once allowed you to do to my brother. I would like to hold a knife to your scrotum.' He put his arm around Turiddu's neck as he sat there. 'But I will not do anything like that at all, because that is what you want me to do, because that is what you would enjoy.'

He held him tight. Turiddu could not speak. He seemed overcome by some powerful emotion. The sight of this was more terrifying than anything Traiano had ever seen. There was a terrible stillness in the room. He could hear his mother breathe. He could feel his own heart racing. Then Calogero seemed to right himself, and held one of Turiddu's arms to the table in an almost affectionate gesture. He employed his left hand to do this, and with his right hand, in one fluid gesture, he brought a knife out of his pocket and rammed it into Turiddu's hand, nailing it to the table.

Anna screamed, while Turiddu whimpered like an injured dog. Traiano's jaw dropped in surprise, and Calogero flashed him a sudden smile.

Calogero looked at Anna.

'You need to get rid of it,' he said.

Then he left.

The hand was patched up. The surgeons at the hospital were very good at dealing with knife wounds, and were used to hearing about how people so often had accidents in the kitchen. It required an operation, though the surgeons said that it he would regain full use of it. That was one mercy, and it was taken by many to be a warning: Calogero had just dealt a flesh wound, painful but not serious; next time he would maim him for life, or even kill him. This wounding was a warning. With this in mind, several well-meaning friends of Turiddu advised him to get the hell out of Purgatory while he still could. They came to the hospital and told him so. Their advice was that he should not even go back to Purgatory to clear out his stuff (whatever he needed could be sent on) but he should go straight to the station, and get the first train north, and not stop until he was in Reggio, Naples or Rome. They urged a new life on the other side of the straits of Messina.

The people who gave this advice were his own family, his tearful mother, and his estranged father, to whom he had not spoken to for three years at least, and who now came to see him. In addition, several of the boys, among them Alfio with the funny teeth, who worked with him for Calogero came and gave the same advice.

Turiddu viewed this advice with distaste. They all seemed a little too eager to get rid of him; his family had never wanted him, ever since he had taken up with Calogero; and as for his associates, once he was gone, they would step into his shoes with the bar, with the drugs. Besides which, he could not leave Anna and their child, the child Calogero had threatened to kill. It was perfectly true that he had quite a bit of money saved up, and could start a new life in Rome or Naples, but he did not want to run away. He did not want to show that he was frightened. The truth was that he wasn't frightened.

192

'This was a warning. Next time he will kill you,' they all said.

'Should I be frightened of him killing me? Why shouldn't he be frightened of me killing him? How many men has he killed? And how many have I?'

The men surrounding the hospital bed were silent.

'Who has done all the work in the quarter?' continued Turiddu. 'Who stole all the wallets? Who evicted the difficult tenants, and threatened those who didn't pay? Who collects the drugs and gives them to you to sell? Who makes sure there is order in the bar? All by the power of my fists and my knife. Who killed Carmine del Monaco? Not him!'

The five men, all of whom made a very good living working for Turiddu, took this in. Perhaps there would be a war between Turiddu and Calogero. In which case whose side would they be on? And who would win? It was essential to be on the winning side, and pick that side early.

'He is jealous of me,' said Turiddu. 'I am a better fighter. I went in and killed del Monaco because I was not afraid.'

But it appeared to them at that moment that Calogero was the cleverer of the two. He had not killed del Monaco. He had not got his hands dirty. He had used Turiddu. He was a better strategist; he thought ahead. It was becoming clearer that if there were to be a war, just who would win.

'He is jealous of me. I screwed Anna and made her pregnant. He can't give his wife a son. He can't even screw her. She spends all her time shopping and wasting money, because she doesn't get what women want. He is not a real man. He's…'

They gestured him to be silent. And then something happened. Turiddu's anger dissolved. He began to cry and sob. Tears rolled down his cheeks.

'I did everything for him. I gave him everything. And this is how he repays me,' said Turiddu miserably.

There would be no war. He would simply have to submit. And as with all surrenders, there would have to be negotiations first.

'You know why I have come,' said Anna.

'I can guess,' said Calogero.

She had come to him at home, and she had been shown into the room he used as a study by Stefania; she had brought Traiano with her. Calogero realised that this was a good move.

'How are you?' he said to the boy.

'Well,' said Traiano.

'Not upset by what I did to Turiddu?'

The boy shook his head.

Anna sat down at Calogero's invitation, and the boy stood next to her.

'Go and give Uncle Caloriu a kiss,' said Anna.

The boy approached Calogero, who was sitting in a large leather armchair. He put his arms around him and kissed his cheek. Then he settled on the arm of the chair, in the crook of Calogero's arm.

'But don't annoy him,' said Anna.

'How could he annoy me?' asked Calogero.

The child returned to his mother.

'Well?' said Calogero. 'Make your request.'

He spoke like a monarch. But he was a monarch.

'I want you to forgive Turiddu.'

'I am not sure I can do that,' he said. 'He's insulted me. I hear things. And even if I could overlook the insult to myself, then I am not sure I could overlook the offence that other people have taken. I am very moderate. Others, less so.'

He inclined his head to one side. She knew that he was talking of Stefania.

'I know there is a long history between you. You have known him since he was eight years old. He has been a great help to you.'

'I hope you are not going to talk to me about gratitude,' said Calogero.

'No, of course not.'

'I gave him a warning. Now he must leave. As for you, you need to think of what you are going to do.'

'The child inside me is innocent,' she said.

'So you told don Giorgio and so he told me. He was here earlier. He threatened to expose me to the Confraternity. Well, the Confraternity cannot do without me. So that is an idle threat. But I do admit it looks bad. Are you sure it is his?'

'Whose else could it be?'

'Think, and let people know that it wasn't him. Just hint that it is someone whose name must remain secret.' He smiled. 'Let us just hope it doesn't look like Turiddu. Let's hope it is a fine child, like Traiano.'

She began to weep with relief.

'Are you going to kill him?' she asked.

'Are you asking me to?'

She shook her head.

'You wouldn't be the first to ask me to do so,' he said. He looked at Traiano. 'Do you want me to kill him?'

The boy looked at him, smiled, and nodded, while his mother blew her nose into a paper tissue.

'Turiddu is not good at making friends,' said Calogero. 'And he is not good at keeping them. But of course I am not going to kill him. What do you take me for? He can come back, he will be perfectly safe, but he has to learn how to behave. You had better explain that to him. He may listen to you. I think he stopped listening to me some time ago. He thought he was too important to take advice. He likes to think that he can command. He cannot.'

'I will tell him,' said Anna. 'The reason I came to you is that he has been good to me and to my son.'

'No, he hasn't,' said Calogero. 'The person who has been good to you and your son is me, and me alone.'

She understood what he meant by this.

'I am grateful,' she said. 'I am grateful for all you have done for us in the past, and for all you are doing for us now, and all you will do for us in the future.'

Calogero nodded. This was the least he could expect, he seemed to say.

'Traiano,' she said, turning to her son. 'I have told you that we owe everything to Uncle Caloriu, haven't I?'

'Yes,' agreed the boy. 'And you told me that if he asks me to do anything, anything at all, I am not to hesitate.'

His mother nodded. She looked at the floor. Calogero smiled. She rose to leave. As they went to the door, the child broke away from his mother, and approached Calogero. He wrapped his arms around his waist. Calogero kissed him on the forehead, ruffled his hair, and wished them a pleasant day.

In hospital, his bandaged hand still throbbing, waiting to be discharged, Turiddu muttered that he was a dead man.

'No,' said Anna. 'He gave me his word that he would not kill you.'

He looked at her pityingly. He was not sure she understood. Calogero had the blessing of Palermo. He could kill him, or have him killed, and Palermo would barely notice. And then he would be replaced; and everything would continue as before. He was expendable. Worse than that, he was someone who should be removed, a reminder of the violent past, a reminder of the days when Calogero's main income had come from the theft of stolen wallets and valuables from churches – a reminder of all that Calogero wanted to forget.

And if that was not all, he was the one who had stabbed Carmine del Monaco, for Calogero. One threw away the knife, because it was evidence; and then one threw away the one who had wielded the knife, because he was evidence as well. Even if he went north, to Reggio, to Naples or to Rome, he would be hunted down and killed because he knew too much.

He looked at Anna. Did she understand this? Could he explain it to her? Could he trust her? Had she in fact, in speaking to Calogero, received assurances to assuage her conscience? Was she in fact prepared to see him killed, knowing that her future without him would be assured? Was she prepared, despite the child in her womb, to throw him overboard, like everyone else?

There were only two avenues left open to him. The last, final avenue was to talk to the police, and tell them everything. But, as Calogero surely knew, this would only incriminate himself; and the police were friends of

Calogero, weren't they? They would not protect him, even if they could protect him. Why should they protect him, when in their eyes, he was just a piece of lowlife scum?

But there was one avenue before that. Not the police, the Church.

'Get don Giorgio,' he said to Anna. 'Tell him it is urgent.'

He would not confess to the police. He would confess to the priest.

Don Giorgio came to the hospital. He had never exchanged words with Turiddu since the time of preparing him for his first Holy Communion, though they had seen each other across the square and in the streets of Purgatory in the intervening ten years, during which Turiddu had turned from a little boy into a hardened criminal. He came motivated by pity and by curiosity. He had already spoken to Anna and found her story incoherent and incredible. Now, he supposed, he would hear the story complete.

Out came the whole story, whole and entire; Turiddu spoke in a low tone, dispassionately, as if he were talking about someone else; as if all this were happening to a third party, and he were just a neutral observer. Most of the story don Giorgio knew, though there were some details of things that had transpired between Calogero and Turiddu in their ten years of association that he had only guessed at.

At the end the priest was thoughtful. Turiddu's sins had certainly found him out, he felt impelled to say. But he knew that, and to remind him of what he surely could not forget, would be, he felt, unkind.

'I am under sentence of death,' he said.

'You must go to the police,' said don Giorgio.

'They would arrest me and I would be found dead in my cell, dangling from a rope, or with my throat cut, as if I had done it myself.'

Don Giorgio knew this was true.

'Go to Reggio, to Naples or to Rome. Start again. You are still young.'

'Calogero would send people after me and kill me,' he answered gloomily. 'He knows that once out of his sight, I would talk. He knows that once away from here I would not feel so frightened of him, and I would talk. There's only one way for my life to be saved. You talk to him. You know the whole story. Get Rosario to go with you; make their reconciliation depend on me being alive.'

'If anyone has cause to hate you, surely it's Rosario.'

'Yes. He must hate me. So must the family of Carmine del Monaco. But Rosario is a good Catholic boy. He knows he has to forgive me. If you tell him to forgive me, he will; and if he forgives his brother on the condition that he forgives me, then his brother will forgive me. You know, Rosario is the one he always loved, not me. That's why he hates me so much, because I separated him from his beloved brother.'

'He mistreated his brother for years, and cheated him.'

'Cruelty is the way he shows love. Why else would he want to kill me?'

'Rosario is in Rome. In a few days he will be coming to stay in Acireale. He will be working for the lawyer Petrocchi. I could tell him to come earlier. Summer is beginning.'

'Will I see autumn?' asked Turiddu.

'I will see what I can do,' said the priest.

Don Giorgio walked from the room they were keeping Turiddu into the hospital forecourt. There he took out his mobile and phoned Rosario. He got straight to the point.

'There is a crisis in Purgatory. It seems that your brother is going to murder his trusted assistant Turiddu.'

'Turiddu?'

'Yes. You sound surprised.'

'I am not. My brother is the sort of person who would murder someone, and Turiddu is the sort of person who would get himself murdered. And that association has probably run its course. It was always going to. You see my brother has grown respectable. And Turiddu did the unforgiveable thing of growing up.'

Don Giorgio said: 'You speak as if you know all about it, as if all of this were bound to happen. But I think we must do something to prevent your brother killing Turiddu.'

'For a lot of the time, I was there,' Rosario reminded him. 'When your protégé turns into your equal and possibly your rival, then the whole thing goes sour. So, it is, as you say, Father, a crisis. What is to be done?'

He explained.

'So soon?' said Rosario. 'Am I to be reconciled with my brother so soon? Do you suppose he impaled Turiddu's hand just to engineer this?'

Don Giorgio was thoughtful.

'It's possible. But he could have waited until he heard you were back in Sicily. I want you to get the next flight or the next train down. But your being reconciled with your brother depends on your forgiving Turiddu. Do you want to save his life? Do you want to forgive Turiddu and ask your brother not to kill him?'

'Is that he only way to stop Caloriu killing Turiddu?'

'If you were reconciled, and then he later broke his promise and killed Turiddu, well, you would be very much taken in, wouldn't you? Turiddu would be safe as long as he needed you. And he does need you.'

'What makes you say that, Father?'

'If you are going to be respectable, then you have to have respectable family relations. The common rumour is that he mistreated you abominably, that he was a brute.'

'He was a brute,' said Rosario. 'He is a brute.'

'But now he needs to hide it,' said the priest. 'It is in his interest to hide it. He has to rewrite that piece of history. He has to turn from brute to gentleman.'

'And I should help him do that?' asked Rosario. 'I know that is what Stefania wants. But is that what you want? For me to help him cover up his true nature? For me to help him appear to be what he is not? To cover up all his crimes?'

'That is not what I want at all,' said don Giorgio. 'That is not what anyone should want. We should all want to see your brother in jail for his crimes. But, there's no evidence, the police have been bought off... the real question right now is do we want to prevent him killing Turiddu? Or do we want him to go ahead and do it? He has fathered a child on this Romanian woman, Anna. Do we want that child to grow up without a father?'

'A father like him?'

'A father like him,' echoed the priest.

He took the night train down from Rome, a journey he had made many times. The train left at 11pm, and trundled southwards through the night as he slept in his comfortless and stuffy couchette. Before dawn the train arrived at Villa San Giovanni and was loaded carefully onto the ferry, carriage by carriage, a process that woke him from his fitful sleep. Then, as the ferry crossed the straits of Messina, he went up to the deck and ate a rice ball and watched the sun come up over the sea. By eight, the train arrived at Catania, and there was don Giorgio, as arranged, waiting for him on the platform.

'Let's get it over with,' he replied to the priest's suggestion that he might want to rest, wash and change. 'I suppose I have to see Turiddu first,' said Rosario. 'Then I shall go and see Caloriu. You will come with me?'

'Of course. But I will be in the background.'

The priest knew that both Turiddu and Calogero would want their moment of drama.

And so it proved.

In the hospital, Turiddu was penitent, tearful and voluble.

'You have don Giorgio to thank,' said Rosario.

Then the three of them went to Calogero's house. The priest and the penitent waited outside. Rosario went in, the door opened to him by Stefania.

She smiled.

'He's been waiting for you,' she said. 'I thought for a moment you would never come. But I am glad to see you. So will he be.'

Alone, Rosario went in to the room Calogero used as his office. He was sitting behind the desk, and he slowly raised his eyes as the door opened, and looked at his brother. Rosario stood before him. Nothing was said.

'I knew you would come back,' said Calogero at last. 'I knew that you would not allow that little bastard to separate us forever. I knew you would not cut yourself off forever.'

Rosario said nothing. Calogero got up and approached him. He walked to where he stood and embraced him.

'Rosario, you broke my heart,' he said, kissing his lips and holding him.

'Did you take the train?' he said at length. 'The night train? You should have flown. It is much more comfortable. You look like you haven't slept much.'

'You are not so slim as you were,' remarked Rosario with a low laugh.

'Almost five years of marriage and my wife's cooking since you saw me last. But now I have got hold of you, I will never let go of you again.'

'I have come to ask you not to kill Turiddu,' said Rosario.

'If you forgive him, then I must forgive him as well, I suppose,' said Calogero. 'But he does not matter anymore. Only you matter.'

'Then if I matter, do not kill him.'

'Everyone assumes that I want to kill him, which may be true, and that I could kill him, which is surely ridiculous.'

'Show the world it is ridiculous by not doing it.'

'Good advice. Call him in, and let us put him out of his misery.'

Rosario went to fetch Turiddu. The priest came too.

'My brother has asked me to forgive you and he wants to assure you that you will never come to any harm,' said Calogero.

'Thanks, boss,' said Turiddu humbly.

He approached Calogero and knelt down in front of him, took his hand and kissed it. Calogero waited for some seconds before telling him to get up.

'Anna will be waiting for you,' he said at length.

Around the quarter, that evening, there was a sense of relaxation. Peace had been made, war averted. Turiddu went to sleep knowing he had avoided death.

Chapter Nine

He wasn't afraid. Calogero had promised not to kill him, and had made this promise to Anna and to Rosario, and to don Giorgio. This meant, Turiddu recognised, precisely nothing. Perhaps Calogero would not kill him, perhaps someone else would. But what difference would it make, given that the result would be the same? He was a dead man walking, a man who would very soon leave this life, a man on death row, whose lawyers might win a stay of execution but who could not in the end avoid the electric chair or the rope or whatever means of execution was planned for him. But he wasn't afraid. Fear was an active emotion, a pulsating tremor in the blood. He felt nothing, nothing at all, just a creeping numbness. It was as if the process of death had already started and that mortality was already creeping through his veins. He was dying already, mortifying very slowly and his death would be a long drawn out process. Calogero was playing with him, enjoying himself, watching the spectacle of life slowly draining away from Turiddu.

The child was born. Turiddu found himself rather surprised by the whole process. He accompanied Anna to hospital, and waited in the corridor when she was in the delivery room, with Traiano by his side; then, when the birth was over, he went in, saw the tiny creature in his mother's arms, and felt nothing at all, except an obscure sense of worry. When this boy grew up, what would they tell him about his dead father? What would the boy think of him? Would he hate him? Or would he make the dreadful mistake of idolising him, as a lost father he had never known?

Anna, he noted, was delighted with her new son, whom she determined would be called Salvatore, the same name as his father, being, as he was, a gift from God. He felt a strange sensation seeing her happiness, which he observed, as it were, from an immense distance. It was as if this had nothing to do with him; and indeed, what had he to do with her? They had often shared a bed, and had on a few occasions engaged in the process that had led to the birth of this child. Those acts of sexual intercourse, so painful and laboured at the time, now seemed devoid of meaning. Anna was a stranger to him now, and all her attention was now transferred to little Salvatore. He had served his purpose. And could he blame her? Not really. She knew what he knew, namely that he was a dead man. She had already moved on the next stage, a life without him.

In the last stages of her pregnancy they had not shared a bed. He had slept in the bedroom of Traiano, who now, at the age of twelve, was delighted with his new brother. Traiano, he knew, had always seen him as an interloper; Traiano worshipped his Uncle Calogero, and felt a corresponding contempt for the man whose hand Calogero had nailed to the kitchen table; just as he, Turiddu, had felt contempt for his own father, whom Calogero had fearlessly beaten up at the age of fourteen. He could feel the boy's disdain for him grow as the boy himself grew older. Consequently, when they took the new baby home, he decided that he could not bear to sleep in the flat any more, but went home to his parents.

The official excuse for this was that the baby cried at night and that he needed peace and quiet; and that the boy Traiano was getting big now and needed his own space. There was some vague talk that they would move to a larger flat eventually. But the desire to get away from Anna and Traiano, and little Salvatore, was fuelled not just by the realisation that they were strangers to him, and in the case of Traiano, hostile strangers; it was also motivated by the desire to go home, to go back to the place he had left some three years previously, to live with Anna the prostitute, who, of course, thanks to him, was a prostitute no more.

He did not as such want to say sorry to his father, or to his mother, or his brothers and sisters, who were younger than him. The form of words that would make an apology seemed meaningless to him. He was coming back, unannounced, to his childhood home because he had failed as an adult. In fact, he no longer wanted to be an adult. He no longer wanted to live with Anna or to be a father to Salvatore. He still went over to her place from

210

time to time, but did not enjoy the experience. He was out of place there. He was out of place in the world. The place where he was least out of place was with his parents, where he had grown up.

The greatest agony was that Calogero was no longer in his life. The person who had dominated his every thought since he had been eight years old had now abandoned him. Every day they had met, every day they had spoken, and now hardly at all. Sometimes he saw Calogero in the streets of Purgatory or else across the square or inside the Church of the Holy Souls in Purgatory, but never once did Calogero look in his direction, never once did he seem to notice his presence. He was not an object of hatred of loathing, but of indifference, which was far worse. He knew that hatred was a love that went wrong; and that the true opposite of love was an absence of any feeling at all. Calogero had filled a large part of his life, and been more important than parents, brothers or sisters or friends. And now, that large part of his life was blank.

At night, in his old bedroom at home, he cried himself to sleep, at first, until he fell into a mood of dull apathy, remembering how in that very room, he and Calogero had first amassed the various things that they had stolen from churches, and the various wallets they had lifted from unsuspecting people in the street, and the other things they had seized by force and the use of a threatening knife. Why had he, from the age of eight, directed by Calogero, then twelve, been such an adept at theft? He had done it because it had been a thrilling game; and also because the idea of money (not that he ever spent much) was always attractive; and because one loved doing something that people thought was wrong and one could get away with.

Calogero had led him to cross all the boundaries. The first had been theft; then had come robbery and with it, the profanity of robbing churches. Then had come the rejection of his father and his authority, and the way Calogero had beaten up his father in front of him. Then had come the thrill, the ecstatic dread, that had come from being taken up by Calogero to Anna's flat, and being told he could have her, while Calogero took Traiano away for an ice cream. Finally, there had come the crossing of the last boundary, when he had calmly walked into the pizzeria and stabbed Carmine del Monaco, with the attendant silence, followed by the screams and shouts of confusion. All done to please Calogero.

He had been, he saw, manipulated. He remembered the huge outpourings of affection, how he would be woken from sleep to find Calogero next to him in bed, with his arms around him, and his breath hot against his neck. He remembered too the equally dramatic withdrawals of affection, when Calogero, at some slight provocation, would pull him by the hair, and beat him with his belt until he bled and begged for mercy. Then mercy would be given. Turiddu knew that this too was a sign of love. He knew too that he was now too old to be beaten in that manner, and that the withdrawal of favour was the equivalent.

The curious emptiness of his life was filled with his work, which consisted in picking up drugs from the pizzeria on Viale Kennedy, and distributing them to certain trusted dealers, and overseeing their sale in the bar Anna managed. Every night the days takings and profits would be totted up, and Calogero would send a boy for his cut of the profits. He also acted as Calogero's rent collector with certain properties, though he was not the only one who did this work. But with his reputation for extreme violence he had the job of collecting from those who were late payers or who needed to be evicted. Given his reputation, most people fled before he turned up, and there were few occasions where he had to administer a good hiding, which usually consisted in throwing the late payer down the staircase, and in the case of the male offenders, kicking them in the balls. Then, when the offender lay groaning at the bottom of the steps, he would casually undo his flies and empty his bladder on them, and, on occasion, shit on them too. But this was called for less and less, and most of the tenants were paying by direct debit, and, when they failed to do so, doing a midnight flit. Some might later have the misfortune to meet Turiddu or one of the other boys, such as Alfio, the one with the teeth, in some other part of the city, where they would not escape punishment.

But the Purgatory quarter was becoming more peaceful, more gentle, and his services of this type needed less.

Violence was something he approached with calculation; in this he knew he was like Calogero. With Calogero there was no anger, rather there was the use of violence and torture as a way of advancing what he wanted. And what he had wanted was to serve Calogero. He remembered the act of violence he had committed against Rosario, how he had subjected him to the water torture and worse. He remembered how Rosario had howled like an animal as they had held him down and as he had held his knife against his scrotum, preparing to slice it open. The point of his knife was pressed against the flesh, and then Calogero had told him to stop. But if he had not been told to stop, he would have continued. Calogero had known that. But he had not known that Calogero would tell him to stop.

It had been a test, like that story in the Bible, when God had asked Abraham to sacrifice his son. Calogero had asked him to cut off Rosario's balls, told him how to do it, and he had been only too willing to show his complete loyalty to the boss. There was nothing he would not do for him. The boss had seen that, and then stopped him. He had not castrated Rosario after all, if that was what the boss had wanted.

The odd thing was he was certain, absolutely certain, that Calogero had only made up his mind at that moment that Rosario was to be spared this final humiliation. Calogero had an almost scientific interest, it seemed to Turiddu, in testing the limits of cruelty. He had told him not to do it not because he thought that doing it was simply too bad a thing to do, but because it was not necessary. The very threat, the knife held to the scrotum, was enough to make Rosario a eunuch forever. Besides, he could if he wanted to at a later date, carry out the threat. So Rosario would spend the rest of his life knowing that his testicles depended on his brother not wanting to cut them off, all the time; that his wellbeing depended on the good wishes, infinitely capricious, of his brother. And just as Rosario had to live with the knowledge that there was nothing his brother would not do to him if he wanted to, so he, Turiddu, had to live with the knowledge that there was nothing he would not do for Calogero if Calogero asked. They both lived in a world governed by the will of Calogero which was held back by no moral law.

The heat of summer increased, and Catania became a furnace, and Purgatory was deserted. Even those who came to buy drugs in the bar seemed to be elsewhere, perhaps at the beaches, perhaps on the cooler slopes of Mount Etna, perhaps somewhere else in Sicily, like Cefalù or Erice, anywhere, but not here, not in this broiling narrow cityscape. One August day, just before the feast of the Assumption, when everything was at its most dead, when trade had ceased, he made his way up to the Anna's place, for the want of anything better to do. It was early evening, and he let himself in the door very quietly, wondering if anyone was at home.

The only sound in the flat came from the low hum of the air conditioner, audible through the partially open bedroom door. The kitchen showed signs of recent use, and he wondered if he should get himself a cold drink from the fridge. Looking through the bedroom door, he felt his heart checked by what he saw there. There was Anna, asleep, breasts bare, lying on her back, uncovered. His eyes were drawn to the sight of her shameless vagina; then to the cradle next to her bed which contained their sleeping child. But he only looked at the child a moment, for next to Anna was Calogero, also asleep, fat, fleshy and naked, with one arm draped over her. And next to Calogero, curled up against him was the figure of Traiano, naked, but awake, and staring directly at him, with defiance in his eyes.

Very quietly, Turiddu turned and left the flat. They had been seen, but, perhaps more significantly, he had been seen. Perhaps he had been meant to see. Could one see such things and live? He was now, he knew, closer to death than he had imagined. That was clear enough. This vision was death, even if he did not understand what it meant. But he now saw how death would come, and he wondered how soon it would be.

After that day, summer retreated, more gracious weather returned to the island and the city, and with it the usual life of Purgatory resumed. As things came to life, he felt the life shrink within him. He withdrew into himself, and spent long hours alone in his bedroom in his parents' flat. Anna saw him no more. She mentioned this to don Giorgio, and don Giorgio once more climbed the steps to Turiddu's parents' home. He sat with the old couple at their kitchen table as he had once before, when Turiddu had been thirteen or so – some seven years ago now. Then he had thought the father old and defeated. Nothing had changed.

'He is not well, he is not well,' was the only thing the father could say.

He spoke as one who had long ago despaired.

'We never see the baby,' said Turiddu's mother. 'We went to see the child, but Anna made it clear that she does not want us. We are Salvatore's grandparents, but that counts for nothing. When Turiddu became a father, we thought it might turn him into a man, a proper man. That Anna was a bad woman once, but even if she has changed…. She was uncomfortable that we were there, and she could not wait for us to leave. It is as though she thinks we bring bad luck.'

Don Giorgio went into Turiddu's room. The young man, though it was hard to think of him as such, was lying on his bed. He motioned to him not to rise. Don Giorgio took a chair and looked around the room. It was a child's room, unchanged, he guessed, since Turiddu had been about twelve years old.

'You are depressed,' remarked the priest quietly.

'Yes,' said Turiddu. 'Most people would be in my situation. My life is over.'

'There is still time to get away,' said the priest.

'How can one get away from oneself?' asked Turiddu. Then he said: 'Anna is pregnant. Again. Did she tell you?'

'No,' he replied, trying not to sound surprised. 'Are you pleased?'

'It is not mine. We have not been together since Salvatore was born. In fact since Salvatore was conceived. I feel sorry for my son. Anna didn't tell me herself. Traiano did. I think she is a little bit ashamed of herself.'

'Three children by three different fathers,' said don Giorgio. 'Well she might be. Who is the father?'

'I am not sure if she herself can be quite certain,' said Turiddu. 'You might like to question Traiano, or you might like to question Calogero.'

'I shall do neither. It is nothing to do with me. Anna is a disappointment to me. And perhaps to you.'

'You can only be disappointed if you have expectations,' said Turiddu. 'I have none.'

'Are you going to spend the rest of your life lying here?' asked the priest.

'Why not?'

'What about your…. your work?'

'Selling drugs?' said Turiddu. 'I am sure you would not encourage me to do that, would you? Do you remember the way we sat together on the steps of the hotel at Calogero's wedding: you, me, Rosario, and Calogero? Rosario was always a nice boy. In those days I was nicer than I am now. But I was already thoroughly bad. I had stolen, or helped to steal, the Spanish Madonna, may she forgive me for that sin. I had stolen numerous wallets and car radios. I thought I was so clever. The week before the wedding, Calogero had taken me up to Anna and ordered her to let me sleep with her. That was the worst thing I ever did.'

'Not killing Carmine del Monaco?'

'If I confessed that to the police and were sent down for it, I wouldn't do much time for it, as I was a child at the time, and the whole thing was planned by someone else. And after all, we only killed him. He suffered a few seconds, then gone forever. Finished. Anna's suffering has been intense. Calogero had her when he was thirteen, and then he made me have her. He made her into a corrupter of children. And she has to live with that. What a punishment. And she has to go on living. I do not have to go on living.'

'Are you going to kill yourself?'

'It did occur to me, but why should I? Father,' he said, 'Very soon it is going to be the 2nd November, the day of the Holy Souls. There will be the procession. Is Rosario coming from Rome for the occasion?'

'He is.'

'And staying a few days?'

'He plans to.'

'Good, I hope to see him.'

He was meant, he was sure, to pass this on, and so he did. In the middle of all the preparations for the feast, he did not forget to tell Rosario on the telephone that when he came down Turiddu wanted to see him. As for the information about Anna, she had been avoiding him, and now he could see why. Her professions of reform had not been of much duration, and this clearly shamed her. Moreover, Traiano was not to be seen in the vicinity of the Church of the Holy Souls either, and perhaps the shame of his mother's misbehaviour had kept him away as well. In fact, the defection of Traiano from the corps of altar boys was remarked on, as coming at a very difficult time, given that the Church's major celebration was now due. But it was only when Rosario appeared, fresh from the overnight train from Rome, that he realised why the other children had been talking about Traiano.

It seemed, Rosario told him, that Traiano had made a girl pregnant.

Don Giorgio was horrified. He tried to calculate the child's age. 'He's ...'

'Thirteen,' said Rosario.

'Holy Mary!' exclaimed the priest. 'And his mother pregnant at the same time. What a family!'

But what exactly Traiano had got up to at the tender age of thirteen was not something they were ever likely to know, thought Rosario, unless one took the old-fashioned approach and beat it out of the boy. Given that Traiano was tall and broad-shouldered and could probably look after himself, there was only one person who would be able to extract the truth from him, and that would be the man he called Uncle Calogero. But Calogero was the one person who did not need to extract the truth, for he certainly knew it, given that the news of this minor scandal in the Romanian family left him unruffled.

This was something that Rosario expressed to Turiddu as they both stood on the Church steps, on the afternoon of the day of the Holy Souls, 2nd November. They had met by chance, and they were both looking across the square towards the figure of Traiano who stood some distance away surrounded by younger boys.

'Your brother knows everything that happens here,' said Turiddu. 'Ask him all about it. Traiano has had his first woman at the age of thirteen. He has probably started on other criminal activities too: the woman was his reward. The next step will be his first murder.'

'Who will he kill?' asked Rosario in disbelief.

'Wait and see.'

'Where is Anna?'

'Keeping to herself. Can you blame her? Her son makes her afraid and ashamed. She cannot face don Giorgio. At least that is how I see it. It is interesting, when you are a dying man, you see things differently.'

'Are you - a dying man?'

'You'll see. Anna was always a prostitute, you know. When you are a prostitute, you don't just sell your body, you sell your soul. She lost her soul at some point, just as I lost mine. This place should not be called Purgatory, but Hell, as it is full of lost souls. But you were lucky, you escaped. Calogero wasn't able to win you over. You always disliked him. I loved him. Anna loved him. Traiano still does.'

Rosario asked a question that had long troubled him:

'Is my brother sexually normal?' he asked.

'I think so,' said Turiddu, considering. 'But he is not really interested in sex. He could have had all the women in the quarter, but he has been faithful to his wife since he met her, and before that there was only Anna, and that was a couple of times, like a test drive. He was young. He has never been interested in sex very much. What fascinates him is cruelty and violence. He likes beating people. You see those kids on the other side of the square? There isn't a single one he hasn't whipped. He used to whip me. He used to whip you.'

'And I hated him for it.'

'And I loved him for it. I took it for a sign of love. I am not sure I was wrong. He loved you, he loved me; I am sure he has never loved Stefania. But he is frightened of her, because he can't hit her. He never hits women. He would never hit his mother, his wife or his sisters. But me...'

'Stop it,' said Rosario. Then he said: 'There's a man called Fabio Volta that I want you to meet.'

'Is he a policeman?'

'No. He is a political researcher. He is the one who thirty years from now will bring down Calogero and all his friends.'

The Mass for the commemoration of All the Holy Souls in Purgatory started at 6pm, and was followed by a procession round the quarter which lasted until about 8pm. Under the cover of this great event, in which the members of the Confraternity took part, wearing their black capes, Fabio Volta met Turiddu in the privacy of don Giorgio's house. At the end of a two-hour conversation, he asked himself what he had learned.

He learned a great deal that was not useful, about the workings of the way Calogero dominated the Purgatory quarter. That followed the pattern of most criminal associations. What interested him was the way that Calogero had the backing of the friends in Palermo, and how they had given him this because of the way he had got rid of Carmine del Monaco for them. But what had del Monaco done to offend Palermo so badly?

That he already knew: it had to do with the policeman Fabrizio Perraino, in part, whose mother and aunt commanded some interest in Palermo; but it also had to do with the fact that Palermo had noticed that del Monaco was a loose cannon who needed disciplining, and in the end, there was only one action they could apply that worked, namely the sentence of death.

Perraino and his mother and his aunt were possible leads to Palermo. After all, if Palermo had got rid of del Monaco at their request, then it followed that they were in Palermo's debt, and Palermo would one day call in the favour. In fact, one had to assume that Perraino was their man, carrying on as normal, but prepared to do their bidding whenever their bidding came.

The blessing of Palermo meant that no one at all would ever dare interfere with the internal running of the Purgatory quarter. That was Calogero's fiefdom, granted to him by the overlords in the capital. No other criminal would ever cause trouble there, and the police would ignore anything that happened there, knowing that it was not worth provoking Palermo. No one wanted to return to the days of out and out war between the friends and the police, the epoch of car bombs, least of all the police, who longed for a quiet life more than most. But, Calogero himself, though enjoying the mandate of Palermo, had only met their representative once. That much Turiddu was able to tell him. And it had taken him years to get their attention, to get them to hire him. That he was their man meant of course that they would use him again, if they needed him, just as the way rich people depended on dustmen to take away the rubbish they created. But Palermo would surely feel about Calogero the way the rich felt about the garbage men: necessary, but beneath their notice. They did not like Calogero, they regarded him, Volta thought, as a necessity they could not do without, but of which they would rather not think. The drugs trade they controlled simply because it was best for them to control it rather than others; it was a matter of public order. They, the friends, were as committed to public order as were the police, because public order meant that one was able to make money.

The big money was not coming from drugs and prostitution and protection: it was coming from other sources; the use of people like Calogero was purely to make sure that ordinary crime did not interrupt the smooth running of the really profitable stuff, which came from the friends' association with elected politicians. But someone like Turiddu knew nothing about that. How could he? Even Calogero knew nothing about that, though Calogero might one day lead him to someone who did. After all, the friends would use Calogero again, that was certain, just as they had used his father. And that might lead him further up the chain, further into the heart of darkness.

One could follow the men, and one could hope that led somewhere; or one could follow the money. In this matter he was less involved, as money was less interesting than human character; the latter required analysis and detection, the other just clever accountants, and the criminals, with the funds at their disposal, had the very best accountants available. On the question of money, Turiddu was able to offer only limited information. The money was channelled through legitimate businesses and legitimate foundations, the most important of which was the Ancient and Most Noble Confraternity of the Holy Souls in Purgatory. This utterly respectable organisation, which boasted several very distinguished members with famous names, had a huge income from various properties in Catania and elsewhere; it also received huge donations from various companies and firms, and it made benefactions to a long list of people every year. All this was in the public domain, or supposed to be. But it was hard to get hold of a reliable list of donors, many of which were shell companies, and a reliable list of beneficiaries, for quite a few of those seemed to be shell companies as well. But one thing was clear: the pay roll and the pension roll of the Catania operation of the friends from Palermo was masked by the Confraternity.

He had advised his political masters that the best way to disrupt the business of the friends would be to shut down, nationalise, or otherwise seize, the assets of the Confraternity. This was what had happened in 1861, on the creation of the Kingdom of Italy: numerous religious institutions, many of which had long outgrown their original purpose, were confiscated by the state. The University of Catania occupied several buildings acquired this way to this day. And after all, what was the Confraternity, these days? Once it had been a bunch of pious souls who had banded together to pray for the faithful departed, and built a small church for the purpose, with a resident priest to say Mass for the Holy Souls in Purgatory, but it had grown into a hugely wealthy holding company for shadowy figures who had nothing to do with religion, masked by a social club that met once a year to pray. But the dissolution of the Confraternity was a nonstarter. It would spark off a huge row between Church and State which no politician wanted; after all, the faithful had votes. It would make the state look positively Jacobin, as well as greedy. It would seem blasphemous to curtail an institution dedicated to the remembrance of the dead. But far more important was the simple fact that the dark forces that currently used the Confraternity would simply move their operation elsewhere. Better, he realised, was to study the Confraternity and see who was paying in, and who was being paid out, and in that way find out who was truly supporting the friends, and who was being supported by them. For that one needed a lawyer inside Petrocchi's office, a lawyer who dealt with all the work to do with the Confraternity. And in a couple of years, Volta was sure, they would have such a lawyer. For Rosario would finish his law degree and return to Catania and be offered a job by Petrocchi, if all went to plan.

But all this was too technical, in a sense, to hold Volta's complete interest for long. All this involved chasing pieces of paper, trawling through computers, and looking out for discrepancies in accounts, and trying to figure out who really lay behind the various companies and firms that paid and received money from the Confraternity's funds. The human side of things attracted him more. The priest and Rosario had told him about the pregnancy of Anna the prostitute and the impending death of Turiddu. This interested him a great deal. A woman becoming pregnant was nothing special, but he was interested in the reaction of the people of

Purgatory to this otherwise usual event. And as for the death of Turiddu, that too was highly unusual, or so it seemed to him.

As November advanced, and as the winter set in, usually the most gracious season in Sicily, with it came a sense of encroaching despair into the Purgatory quarter. At the beginning of summer, they had all heard that Calogero had forgiven Turiddu, at the intercession of don Giorgio, his brother Rosario and Anna the former prostitute. And yet, though this had come as a relief, there hung about Turiddu the stench of the grave. He had done something wrong, he had insulted the boss, and he would die for it, even if the boss said he would not kill him. The gods who presided over the quarter would ensure he would not live. Turiddu was like a cursed man, some deadly thing had fastened upon him, from which he would not recover. He was like an ancient soldier struck by a poisoned arrow, the venom of which very slowly but irreversibly made its way through his veins. There could only be one outcome. And because they all instinctively believed this, they all abandoned the condemned man. No one would touch him, for it was believed that the curse of death was contagious.

The person who believed this most of all was Turiddu himself. He was convinced he was to die, and he had told Volta so. Moreover, he had an idea of who would kill him, and told Volta this as well. As a child he had had a book of myths and legends, and he knew that when one had a vision of the gods, after that one could not live.

Volta had discussed this with Rosario, one evening in Acireale, before he flew back to Rome. Rosario knew the idea that Turiddu was referring to. In the Bible it said that no one could see God and live; in the lied of the Nibelungs, the warrior who saw a Valkyrie knew that he was soon to die; and amidst the Greeks there were certain unfortunates who had glimpsed the gods in a way they should not have, and been punished with death. Men who violated the sanctuary, or who reached out profane hands to touch what belonged to the gods alone, also were doomed to die.

But Rosario had been dismissive of this.

'My brother stole the Spanish Madonna, with Turiddu's help, and that was certainly a case of unholy hands touching what is sacred. And they stole numerous precious objects from churches in the city. And yet my brother flourished, particularly when he gave the Madonna back, even when he used a murder to cover up the theft. So the idea of being cursed by the gods does not apply to everyone.'

'But these superstitious ideas are not logical,' said Volta.

It struck him, viewing the situation from afar, that Turiddu would feel accursed, and had prepared himself for death; he was a public sacrifice whose death would bring peace and expiation to the quarter. And as the quarter prepared itself for a death, it also prepared itself, with foreboding, for a birth. Anna the former prostitute had given up work and retired to her flat, never emerging. It was as if she were waiting for the death of Turiddu before she could come out with her child. Or was she waiting in silent horror for the child itself – because the rumour had taken root that the child she was bearing was thing of horror.

Anna had made no announcement about the father of the child. It was widely believed that it could not be Turiddu. Dead men were not fertile, and Turiddu himself had said it was not him. It was whispered that the father might just be Calogero himself, but this thought was immediately put aside when it was made known that Calogero did not simply deny it, but would be dismayed that anyone should think so. Besides, there was Stefania to think about. She was adamant that this child of the prostitute was nothing to do with her husband; though, at the same time, it was given to be understood that Calogero did have something to do with the conception and some secret knowledge of the child's origins. The boy

Traiano, now a young man by his own claim, strode around Purgatory, full of the knowledge that he had the boss's confidence. The official story was that Anna had been impregnated by a man whose identity she no longer remembered. But underneath this idea wriggled the horror that the child inside her was the product of incest, and that Traiano had fathered it at the insistent order and with the encouragement of Calogero.

Incest, remembered Volta, was a privilege of the gods of old. It was a sign that they were exempt from human law.

Then just as winter was drawing to a close, it was announced that Anna had miscarried. A few days later she was seen once more in the quarter, in the bar, at her job, looking tired and pale and unhealthy but nevertheless alive, if reticent.

The year turned and the stage was now set for the last act. Rosario was in Rome, but Volta watched, and kept Rosario informed. In May Calogero decided that he would go to Giardini Naxos for a long weekend, and stay at one of the hotels there. He proposed to take his wife and daughters, and with them spend some lazy time by the beach. It was early in the season, and as a result the place was not crowded. On the Sunday after a long and leisurely lunch overlooking the sea, he drove the family back to Catania. The car was parked, and Stefania unpacked their stuff when they got home, and settled their two daughters for the evening. He heard these domestic female sounds from the room next to the one he habitually used; he stood by the window, and looked out onto the square and onto the Church of the Holy Souls in Purgatory, with its elegant dome. After a time, he saw what he was expecting to see. It was Traiano, standing on the church steps in the dusk. He left the room and went down to the square, carefully shutting the street door behind him. There were few people about, even though it was not late. He walked to the steps. Traiano turned towards him as he approached, his face impassive. He was almost as tall as the boss, now, and he had only just passed his fourteenth birthday.

'Well?' he asked, with very slight impatience.

'It is done.'

'How?'

'He hanged himself. In his parents' house, last night, in the middle of the night. In his bedroom. You remember it was an iron bedstead? He tied a belt around his neck and tied one end to the bedstead and hanged himself.'

'Is that even possible?' asked Calogero.

'Very possible. People do it in prisons all the time. You turn the bed upright. It is not a nice way to go. That way or on the door knob. I am surprised you did not know that, boss.'

'I am sure I did,' he said, with a slight smile.

'Well, it happened. His father found him. He died about midnight, and the father must have found him in the morning. There was a big commotion. There were lots of people coming in and out of Church and they called don Giorgio, then they called an ambulance, and then finally they called the police. But of course he had been dead for hours.'

'The key to the flat?'

'I threw it down one of the drains,' said Traiano.

'Well done. I will give you something nice for this.'

'No need,' said Traiano. 'The deed was reward enough in itself. You should have seen the terror in his eyes at the end. I was too strong for him. I have never enjoyed myself so much. I hated him. Revenge is the greatest pleasure, and a revenge that has to be waited for even more so. He called my mother a prostitute and accused her of prostituting me. I had to kill him for that.'

'Well, she was a prostitute, you know, when you were little,' said Calogero.

'I know that. But I minded him telling me that. It was true; if it had not been true, I would not have minded. But it was true and he knew it, and so I had to kill him. Besides, you wanted him dead.'

'Me? I was in Giardini Naxos.'

'Of course.'

'And where were you?' he asked.

'I was making love to my new girlfriend in her bedroom at her house until midnight, when her parents asked me to leave. Then I went home to my house and got there just after midnight. My mother was up with the baby. She knows I came in at that time.'

'Just as the baby's father was dying. How ironic. May he rest in peace.'

'Amen,' said Traiano.

Calogero walked away. He made his way up to his own house, where his wife was waiting for him. He did not explain his absence, and he saw at once that she knew. Someone had phoned her or messaged her with the news that Turiddu was dead. She was clearly satisfied to hear this news, which, her demeanour seemed to suggest, she had long waited to hear.

A month later, with the coming of summer, Rosario returned to Catania. Before seeing his brother, he called at the house where Turiddu had died, to condole with his parents, people he barely knew. But he had been at school with their son. They sat at the kitchen table, and the parents lamented what had happened to them. Their other children were growing up, so they were leaving Purgatory. They had spent their entire lives there, but the house in which they lived was haunted by their son's memory, and made intolerable by the fact that he had died there. Calogero had, through a third party, offered to buy it off them; that made moving easier. Don Giorgio had been very kind, but the funeral had been sparsely attended. They had laid Turiddu to rest in the municipal cemetery where they too would one day lie. Mortality overshadowed them. It had been the father who had found the body. He was haunted by the picture of his son's tortured face. There had been no peace in that death. But there was no doubt that it was suicide in their minds. Their son had been depressed for a very long time. They had tried to do everything in their power to help him. But they had failed.

He went to see don Giorgio.

'It was very nasty. They called me at once. I saw him hanging there, from the end of the bed; the bed was upright. He had used a belt. He must have desperately wanted to kill himself. His face was horribly disfigured. Please, dear God, may I never see anything like that again. He was a wicked man who found no redemption. Hardly a man at all. A child.'

'Are you sure it was suicide, Father?' asked Rosario.

'In this place,' said the priest, 'Nothing is what it seems. It looked like suicide. He was severely depressed. But…. If it wasn't suicide it was meant to look like it; the police came, but they asked no questions. I am sure that lots of people are very glad he is dead. Poor boy. His poor parents. He may not have been much, but he was their son.'

'And he leaves a child, with Anna the Romanian,' said Rosario. 'His parents are leaving. I just saw them.'

'So is Anna,' said don Giorgio. 'And taking the baby. She is going to Syracuse, I think. She says this place is too sad for her now. Your brother is helping her with the costs of leaving. And he is very kindly looking after her. He has bought a small hotel there and she is going to manage it. It is six or seven rooms, a guest house, but it will give her a place to live, a place to live a quiet life.'

'Perhaps that is best,' said Rosario.

'And you, are you going to come back, after you have finished your degree in Rome?'

'I don't know,' he said.

Rosario walked across the square to where his brother lived. The street door buzzed and swung open, and he walked up to the first floor where the front door of the flat was open. His brother's voice called from inside.

He went in.

'Stefania and the children are not here,' said Calogero cheerily. 'Just as well. We were expecting you one of these days. This fellow has been wicked,' he said, indicating the person sitting next to him on the sofa.

It was Traiano.

'I plead ignorance, extreme youth and inexperience,' said Traiano, squirming. 'You have to forgive me, boss. Though really you are not the injured party.'

There was a bottle of vermouth in front of them, the very sweet type, that children found palatable.

'Help yourself,' said Calogero to his brother. 'And maybe we should ask Rosario to judge. What should we do with this little rascal?'

'It depends on what he has done,' said Rosario, pouring himself some vermouth, which was ice cold, straight from the freezer.

'Yeah,' said Traiano. 'It is not that bad. It is what everyone does. It was more her fault than mine.'

'I am still going to give you a good beating,' said Calogero with a smile. 'It is what you need. It never did me any harm, and it never did Rosario any harm.'

'Aw, boss,' said Traiano. 'I have had plenty of beatings in the past, and look at me now. It has done me no good at all. I am beyond redemption. Ask Rosario, I am sure he sees it. But if you want to beat me, please go ahead. My father is in jail in Romania, so you are the only person who can do it, as you are like a father to me.'

Traiano rubbed his dark curly head against Calogero's shoulder.

'Shall I beat him?' Calogero asked his brother.

'No,' said Rosario. 'What has he done?'

'You tell him,' commanded Calogero.

'Six weeks ago, I was caught in bed with a girl by her father. It was the very night poor Turiddu hanged himself. And now the girl thinks she may be pregnant. She is overdue. So, you see, everyone thinks I have been very bad.'

'As it happens the family lives in one of my properties. So I have given them a rent holiday for the next eighteen years, provided they do not make a fuss. When he is eighteen he can marry her if he wants to. No, when he is seventeen. I was seventeen when I married.'

'And Stefania was pregnant, Turiddu told me, he was there. I was there too, but too young to realise.'

'They grow up fast round here,' said Calogero.

'You asked for my opinion,' said Rosario. 'Send him to Syracuse with his mother. And with his little brother.'

The atmosphere changed.

'She does not want me,' said Traiano shortly.

'Can you blame her?' asked Calogero.

'Why not? You're her son,' said Rosario.

'If this girl is pregnant, which she may be or may not be, he has responsibilities here,' said Calogero.

'And the boss needs me,' said Traiano.

'One of these days I am going to beat the hell out of you,' said Calogero with an indulgent smile. 'By the way,' he said, turning to Rosario. 'Stefania is pregnant. That is certain. She has done the test. But tell no one for now. I hope it will be a boy. It is still very early. It happened around the time we went to Giardini Naxos for the weekend.'

'Around the time Turiddu died?'

'Yes. At the same time he committed his sin,' he said gesturing towards Traiano. 'In this place, death and life intermingle. And you, you are back? Another summer living in Acireale, and working with the lawyer Petrocchi?'

'Yes.'

'And then next summer you will be back for good?' asked Calogero almost casually.

'I don't know,' said Rosario.

There was silence. Calogero was thoughtful. He gestured Traiano to leave. He kissed the boss's cheek, got up, crossed to Rosario, embraced him, and then left. The door clicked behind him.

'Turiddu is dead,' said Rosario.

'So they tell me. Good thing too. He had outlived his usefulness. He saw that himself, poor fellow. So he left us. Anna too is leaving us. Though not in so definitive a way. But it is tidier that way. But you, you need to be here.'

'Why? Why do I need to be here?'

'Petrocchi likes and trusts you. The same goes for don Giorgio. You are nice and clean. I can use someone like that.'

'You have said it. You want to use me.'

'If I am dishonest, you do not like it. If I am honest, you complain as well. Of course I want to use you. And in the process you will benefit immensely. That is how the world works. Mutual benefits.'

'You killed Turiddu. You said you would not.'

'What do you care about Turiddu?'

'Nothing. But I care about you lying to me. You killed him.'

'I was in Giardini Naxos at the time, miles away. And I did not creep back in the night to kill him.'

'You killed him, and you used Traiano to do it. And he has the same alibi as you did when you killed Vitale. You were in bed with Stefania at the time. He was in bed with his girlfriend. You killed Carmine del Monaco, and you used Turiddu to do that.'

'There are certain things best left unsaid,' said Calogero quietly, putting down his glass. 'Why dredge up the past?'

'Turiddu has been dead six weeks. It is hardly the past.'

Calogero shrugged.

'What if I were to start digging in your past?' he said. 'What would I find? You do not talk to your own mother. Every day she longs to hear from you, and so do your sisters. And you have ignored her for the last five years. And here you are, so moral, turning your back on family, the only thing that matters.'

Rosario could see that his brother was angry.

'I will go and see our mother today. You are right. I should forgive her. If I forgave Turiddu…. But if you look in my past, you will find nothing. Nothing at all. As you yourself just said, I am clean.'

Calogero stood up, and put down his glass. His brother stood too.

'The night we heard our father was dead, I went out with Stefania and then took her back home and went to bed with her; that was when we conceived Isabella. Then I left, deliberately waking her up, and drawing her attention to the time. Then I went to Via Vittoria Emanuele, where

Vitale was not surprised to see me, as I had told him I would come and see him if I had anything to report. He opened the door to me and I stabbed him. I went out the back, changed clothes, then put the rucksack and the bloodstained clothes next to Vitale and set them on fire with the petrol I had brought with me. Then I left and threw the baseball cap into a public bin in the Cathedral square. Then I came home, waking you up, and telling you the time. It was the most memorable night of my life. And yes, I organised the murder of del Monaco; and yes, Traiano killed Turiddu, he had long wanted to do so, and I gave him permission. But you know why none of this should matter to you?'

'Why?' asked Rosario.

'Because I am your brother.'

'And at last you are telling me the truth,' said Rosario.

'From now on, I always will,' said Calogero. He seized him in his arms and held him close.

Rosario kissed him.

He left the flat to go and see his mother. On his way, he stopped in the Church of the Holy Souls in Purgatory. He stood in front of the Spanish Madonna for a few moments. He was setting out on a dangerous path. But he would, he felt, be protected. That evening he would be seeing Fabio Volta. He would tell Volta that he was in, he had one foot in the door, that he had begun the long slow penetration of the Mafia.

Printed in Great Britain
by Amazon

47386341R00138